Alice Dippleblack in

A War of Steel and Stone

By
K. J. Bailey

Second Edition

This is a work of fiction. Names, characters, places, and incidents either are the products of the author's imagination or are used fictitiously. Any resemblance to actual persons, living or dead, businesses, companies, events, or locales is entirely coincidental.

ISBN: 978-0-9997627-0-7

Chapter 1
A New Threat

Confident atop their horses, three men stride out to the center of what will be the day's battlefield. At their backs stands an army of hundreds, many among them battle hardened veterans of the Blood War. As if having such an experienced force wasn't enough, the enemy is vastly outnumbered. Forced to retreat from the village they terrorized, the villains now stand pinned between a superior force and the great crags of the Gadara Mountains. It seems the enemy found it easy enough to face peasants but when challenged by soldiers, they fled with all haste and have now trapped themselves.

"Think they'll parley?" asks one rider, a young Lobovan noble in ornate, steel, plate armor, shiny and new.

"Have to now," answers the deep gruff voice of an older Echanian, his plate dented and stained from years of use. The commander. "No where for the scum to run."

The third among them is silent. The Murin, not

as imposing as the other two in his leather armor and atop a smaller steed, observes the enemy with a small hand shielding sharp eyes against the high sun.

Despite having fled the moment the army had found them, the unimpressive ranks of the strange invaders now stood facing overwhelming odds without the panic one would expect. Larger than even an Urock, the less than two dozen enemy troops stand in a simple line on a steep slope with backs against an incline of impassible rock, as unmoving as the stone their armor appears to mimic.

Unknown raiders had struck cities in northern Arsalia several times in the last years. These isolated attacks, occurring months apart and only happening at night, had always been as quick as they were devastating, leaving little to identify who was responsible. Of the crazed stories given by witnesses, all accounts at least agreed that the attacks were carried out by enormous men with strength to match their size. Several other accounts say the men were made of stone, though this was dismissed as the wild fantasies of frightened townspeople shaken from sleep. The idea that stone men could even exist was absurd. But the damage done was evidence enough that someone was attacking the kingdom. A coalition force was assembled to deal with the problem and now, finally, the raiders had made the mistake of striking during the day long enough for the army to challenge them.

The three officers wait impatiently for the supposedly stone men to send representatives but none step forth.

"Hah, so fierce were they in smashing farm houses," the Echanian commander mocks, "Now look at them. Too cowardly to even speak. We will end this quickly."

As the horse and wolf men turn their mounts back, the Murin says, "I would advise caution, my lords. We know little of the enemy's true capabilities."

The Lobovan looks back, gesturing negligently with a hand, "They've the high ground, true, but what of it? Our numbers far outweigh such an advantage. It is as Lord Blackburn says, they've no where left to run. Let us put a stop to these raiders already."

The Murin turns to follow his counterparts but continues observing the enemy over his shoulder. His eyes go wide as something emerges from the raiders. A large object is sent sailing high into the air and growing with alarming speed. The Murin has only the time to shout, "LOOK OUT!" before a massive boulder smashes into the Echanian with such force that the commander's body sticks to the stone, rolling along with it, even as the boulder tumbles on toward the soldiers' ranks. The Lobovan's mount rears, shrieking in terror, sending the armored wolf noble clattering to the ground.

The Murin manages to keep control of his own pony and dashes back to his men, shouting, "Archers! Mages!"

The call echoes down the Arsalian army's lines and archers take positions ahead of the infantry along with small groups of robed figures. The Lobovan, abandoned by his mount, flees for the safety of his army as more boulders are sent skyward by the raiders. The unsettlingly high whistle of their flight has many soldier frozen as they watch their death's approach. The boulders don't have the range to reach them initially, but as they crash to the earth, sending up great plumes of dust, the slope of the mountains' foot aids them in rolling into the Warm Blood army. Men break formation to flee from the boulders, sowing confusion into the rest.

"Hold the lines!" orders the Murin officer. Immediately the message is sent down. Groups of Urocks and other soldiers manage to stop of few of the boulders, though many go unchallenged into tight troop formations, crushing and scattering men.

The hail of boulders continues for only a moment but is enough to give the army pause. The dust kicked up in the attack slowly reaches over the Arsalians, blocking their view of the enemy. Many go silent and still, ears perked to listen for the sound of more boulders over the cries of the wounded. Though instead of whistles, they hear as much as feel the earth begin to rumble. As the dust settles the rumbling only grows.

Peering through the thick cloud, the Murin officer is alarmed to find that the ranks of the raiders have swollen, now several times their previous number though still greatly dwarfed by the Arsalians. The moment he sees this he calls,

"Archers, a volley!"

Orders are shouted for those armed with bows to knock, aim, and loose. A wave of arrows arches over the dust wall but lands well short of the enemy lines. The raiders only look on silently, unimpressed.

"Mages!" the mouse officer shouts, "Rain fire on them!"

The small groups of mages standing at intervals along the lines begin collecting the heat of the sun from the ground and air. The temperature drops noticeably, so much so that even this early in summer, the soldiers' nervous breaths show before each of them. The heat is focused and added to by each group of mages, channeling it into massive balls of flame between and over them. They then hurl the fire with a synchronized swing of their arms, sending it roaring up to fall upon the raiders. All watch expectantly as the great fire balls fly in long arcs toward their targets. But the raiders are not interested in waiting to be showered in flames. They charge.

The enemy gives no war cry, their attack accompanied only by the unsettling rumble of many heavy feet and a slight shake in the ground. Seeing the fire balls streak over without effect as the enemy rushes fearlessly into overwhelming odds, the slope lending them speed belying their size, the Murin noble orders, "Infantry!"

The call repeats down the lines as armored men step forth, the mages and archers retreating behind shields, spears, and swords. The Lobovan noble, having rejoined the Murin, calls for a second volley. Archers loose arrows and exhausted mages lend a few bolts from enchanted rings. The Arsalian army looks on expectantly as the raiders are struck... and keep coming. Arrows shatter harmlessly against the raiders' strange armor, though the fire and lighting set on them fair a little better. The soldiers watch as a bolt of lightning cleaves off a leg from one raider, sending it tumbling to the ground. Another hit by fire catches, burning strangely green before losing an arm. But those damaged by the magical assaults are few, far too few.

Officers shout for shield wall formations. Soldiers begin grouping tightly together with shields raised and spears extended, bracing before the individual raiders quickly closing on them. Still silent in their approach, the charging raiders make no effort to avoid these, some even veering toward them. Thick, gray arms rise before their chests and like living battering rams, the mad raiders smash into the ranks of Arsalian soldiers. The thunderous crashes of steel on stone resound over men screaming and shouting.

Officers order, "Hold 'em!" as the second and third lines of infantry rush to join the first. Then the fourth, and fifth. The Murin watches from atop of small hill with his Lobovan counterpart, open mouthed as the raiders display unimaginable strength. The warriors carry no weapons, merely swinging massive arms about with force enough to send fully armored men flying back by the handful and into their own while flattening those unfortunate enough to fall before them.

Still, the Arsalian army has numbers many times the raiders' own and have them quickly surrounded. Steel sings loudly along with the chorus of men shouting as axe and sword bite into the raider's strange, stony armor from all directions. The armor chips away not to reveal the flesh hidden beneath but only more stone. The Murin watches a roaring behemoth of an Urock bring down his great hammer on a raider's shoulder with enough force to shatter the weapon's thick handle. The raider staggers, it's shoulder crumbling under the blow, the arm simply dropping off. But the raider still does not cry out. It only rights itself and turns to the Urock, who looks down in confusion at his broken weapon. The raider then raises it's other fist high before bringing it crashing down atop the bear soldier's head, his steel helm yielding as if only soft dough under the power of the blow.

"Impossible," murmurs the Lobovan noble, having acquired another horse, "These are not men."

The Murin only looks on in disbelief as each of the raiders take an absurd number of strikes, magical and physical, to finally fall. Even while their numbers diminish those that remain do not lose heart but appear to only grow all the more powerful, swinging with new speed and zeal. The last and largest of them fights with such mad strength, tossing away soldiers with the careless ease of a dog shaking off water, that the Murin must take action. Pointing a single finger at the raider, he carefully takes aim before calling, "Rairak!"

The ring on the mouse noble's finger glows an

azure blue and for one brilliant moment, an arch of vicious lightning links the Murin's finger to the great raider's head, causing the latter to burst in a shower of rock. Immediately, the raider crumbles into a pile of rubble.

The men, nervously at first, begin raising their weapons to cheer their victory.

"Not *so* tough then," remarks the Lobovan noble, grinning to the relieved army.

"I wish to see these raiders," says the Murin, who then leads his mount forth to investigate the ruin of the enemy.

The cheering soldiers part before the nobles as shouts of "Make way!" are thrown about. A few men are examining the headless fallen raider and the Murin dismounts to join them. All that remains are rocks and stones of varying sizes.

One man, poking around the rubble with the shattered haft of a spear, looks up in a mix of fear and bewilderment, "My lord. There was nobody inside."

The stones are stained deeply with Arsalian blood though inspection of the fallen raider reveals that what was taken as strange armor, isn't armor at all, but the body of these creatures.

"Some trick," says the Lobovan, still atop his horse, "They are fallen at least."

Before anyone can say more, the earth begins to shake around them and frightened eyes search for a new threat.

Above them, a mountain comes to life.

In Arsalia's capital of Eledon, a large fist slams on a round, wooden table with a resounding echo. It's owner, a Leonain, roaring with strength despite advanced years, "HOW!?" at the news that the northern coalition force had been defeated. "Lord Blackburn's army was ten times and more the size of the enemy!"

The handful of other elaborately clothed individuals, accustom to the Leonain's boisterous outbursts, wait to hear more from the one among their number reading the most recent news from the north. "Lord Blackburn... was killed," the reader announces with surprise, to the shock of his counterparts.

"What of Lords Alvaro and Danior?" asks a white furred Lagomorph.

The Rotan holding the message reads on before saying, "They have taken position in Boreadon with their remaining forces."

"Fled you mean," grumbles the Leonain.

The lion man gets a few dirty looks and the Rotan continues, "Lord Alvaro claims the enemy they faced were made of stone given life. He requests immediate reinforcement, stressing the need for mages."

Others begin to murmur and the Leonain rumbles, "Lost an army fighting rocks?"

Over them the Rotan reads, "He says a *titan* appears to be leading them." He then tosses the rolled up note to the table, letting the many eager hands of the others reach for it as those assembled relate their disbelief.

"Impossible," growls the Leonain, "There's not even been the sighting of a titan in Arsalia, *or* bloody Feoria, in the age of seven kings!" Others agree and the Lion man adds, "Covering for their failure no doubt."

"And what of these 'stone men'?" the Lagomorph curiously asks his counterparts.

"Golems, the mages call them," comes the voice of a mature woman, just slipping into the chamber in elaborate robes that drag the ground at her feet.

"You're late. We've a possible crisis, maybe even another war, and you're late," grumbles the Leonain.

The robed Didel extends her sleeved arms out, "Apologies my lords. But the winds were singing and I simply had to listen."

"Golems, Lady Huld?" asks the white rabbit man.

As the opossum woman takes a seat left for her, she answers, "Indeed. Apparently, golems are beings of earth and magic as we are flesh and blood."

"Magic," the Leonain says distastefully.

"Can they be stopped?" asks the Lagomorph.

"Certainly," nods Lady Huld, "As each of us needs blood, so too do golems need magic. Rid them of this and they will fall."

"A mage fuels them then. Kill it and the fiends will perish," asserts the Rotan.

"A relief, but what of this titan? If it in fact *is* behind them," the Lagomorph wonders.

"There is no titan," the Leonain assures, "They are gone from our lands."

"But Lord Alvaro's missive..." counters the Lagomorph.

The Leonain raises his maned head, "Meaning no offense to the Murin people, but many things likely look more imposing in their eyes."

"Lord Alvaro is not the type to exaggerate," interjects the Rotan, "I believe it would be wise for us to heed his words."

"Even if there is a titan *somehow* leading these raids, what of it? We've beaten titans before, we can do it again," the Leonain grumbles irately.

"We'd dragons then," reminds the rabbit man, "And, if I recall correctly my history, even with them, the battles against the titans were hard fought."

The Rotan raises an eyebrow, "A shame we've no dragons left."

Lady Huld lifts a finger, "There *is* one."

"You refer to the Dippleblack girl?" asks the Lagomorph, more a comment than a question.

"A mere child. She is no warrior," says the Leonain dismissively.

"A child who has the loyalty of the only dragon left in all our lands," remarks the robed Didel.

"We cannot afford to recklessly throw armies

away," adds the Lagomorph, "The peace with Feoria is too fragile. If the girl and her dragon can end the northern threat without the need to divert strength from the border territories, I believe it would be to our benefit."

The Rotan nods, "I agree. Did we not allow her to keep the young dragon specifically for such a purpose?"

"What have we to lose," the Leonain shrugs, "Riders will be dispa-"

Lady Huld interrupts with another raised finger, "I have already taken the liberty of sending for her myself."

Chapter 2
Life

Alice Dippleblack waits anxiously atop a large rock at the edge of a great forest. The Tokala had only arrived last night on her dragon, Squiggles, and had just placed the white stone inside the hollow of the tree before dawn that morning. Even so, the young vixen fidgets with her thickly furred, sunset orange tail, telling herself again and again that it will be a while before Danahlia has a moment to check the tree. Still, every flutter of a bird, hop of a squirrel, or rustle of a breeze has her scanning around for her Liguna. When she doesn't see her, Alice goes back to thinking of all that had changed.

The Blood War was over. After years of fighting it took an unusually long winter to finally convince the warm blooded Arsalians and the cold blooded Feorians that the conflict between them was not worth the cost to their people. Or was it? In truth, Alice didn't know why the war had stopped. Did enough people die? Was it too expensive? Were enough homes burned? Are enough children without parents? Was it all? Was it none? She wasn't sure. All Alice really knew is that it's end finally allowed for her and her father to return to

Arsalia.

Once she was reunited with her farther, long thought claimed by the war, Danahlia's uncle had them kept in the great city of Ter'Bour. A Cold Blood city wasn't terribly different from a Warm Blood one. Their were homes, businesses, temples, and lots of people. The big difference there was that Alice and her father were outsiders. Many Feorians did not care to see Warm Bloods in their city. This meant the Tokala rarely left their accommodations. Still, it was never boring to live among the Cold Bloods. On many days, warriors would arrive to study foreign combat techniques from Alice's father, known to them as Robert the Red.

Robert Dippleblack was a firm believer in learning through experience, thus lessons most often had him being challenged by the warriors one, or sometimes several, at a time. Alice had never seen her father fight in earnest and is fairly sure she still hadn't, even when facing multiple opponents. While sparring, Robert Dippleblack was swift yet precise, powerful yet yielding. If an opponent charged, he would often let them, moving around the attack as if only air before striking vital areas with the speed of a viper. If an opponent kept on the defensive, he would mock them and leave himself open until frustration forced an attack. He would redirect and evade blows rather than block them, letting his opponents waste precious energy striking the air and ground while he conserved his own until an opening presented itself. Even as his pupils improved, Alice's father only seemed to get faster, as if only letting just enough of his ability show to give him the edge.

Alice trained with the warriors too. She was nowhere near her father's level, but seeing what he could do inspired her greatly. The warriors were always bigger and stronger than she but her father would say, "If you can't match their size and strength, you have to beat their wit and speed."

Alice practiced hard every day, her naturally lithe body making her a small target and with training, a faster one. Even so, she took her share of hits. They only ever used blunted weapons but they still stung and bruised. When she did, her father would say, "That's good. Now you know what it feels like to get hit. So next time, don't." Under her father's tutelage, Alice managed to improve her skills dramatically in these years and when the time came, she returned to Arsalia a confident swordswoman.

The end of the war also saw Danahlia married. As Alice was not allowed to leave Ter'Bour while the conflict was still being waged, Danahlia had remained close to Alice. When they were not together, the Liguna was generally away with Squiggles, searching for their friend, Twinkaleni, whom they'd not heard from since parting ways. Danahlia had found evidence that suggested Twinkaleni had visited the caves the girls had lived near in the Gadara Mountains but no trace of the Murin mage herself. Once the war was over, in an effort to strengthen the new peace, Danahlia, coming from the Cold Bloods' prominent Ashclaw clan, was wed to an Echanian noble from a Warm Blood house of similar standing. She was Lady Chevell now.

Alice was not invited to the wedding, since it would have been improper for a peasant to attend such an important ceremony, but Danahlia did have letters sent to her inviting her to visit. The Chevell estate was in the far western part of central Arsalia. Fortunately, flying atop a dragon made the distance a minor issue. The first time Alice had visited Danahlia at her knew home, she was shocked to see the Liguna in a dress. It was a purple frilly thing and not at all in line with the lizard girl's taste. Still, she did look lovely in it, strange, awkward, and uncomfortable, but lovely. Her new husband was nice too, tall, fit, and handsome. Formal visits were pleasant but not nearly enough for the Tokala and Liguna to really enjoy each others company, as they were almost always attended on these and didn't get any time alone. So the pair took to meeting in secret.

At the edge of the vast country estate, there is a tree with a hollow were a branch had rotted off at some point. Inside it is a single white stone. The stone is not uncommon, but by placing the stone in the tree, Alice could signal Danahlia that she was waiting for her. Each day, Danahlia would check the tree under the guise of taking a leisurely stroll. If the stone was in the hollow, Danahlia would remove it, placing it among some others on the ground. She would then go looking for Alice at their secret meeting spot, a large rock at the edge of the forest bordering the Chevell estate. This was where Alice waited now.

It took a while sometimes. Edward Chevell, Danahlia's husband, would frequently accompany the Liguna on her walks, making breaking away to check the tree difficult. Since Danahlia's marriage to him was in an effort to strengthen the fledgling peace between Arsalia and Feoria, and it was impossible for children to come from such a union, it was very important that the pair looked the happy couple. This was a key reason Danahlia and Alice had to keep their love a secret. Alice flying around at night atop a dragon was another. It was nice that Danahlia didn't live all the way in Feoria, but Alice wonders if she is happy here. If any of those hastily married and sent to live in foreign lands could find happiness in their new lives. Alice is thinking about this, fiddling with the white fluff ending her tail, when she hears a rustle behind her.

She looks to find a fist sized stone tumbling through the grass. Knowing what this might mean, Alice jerks her head forward again to find Danahlia running toward her from some bushes.

"Danny!" Alice cries, leaping off the rock to fling herself toward her Liguna.

Danahlia flies toward her in a fanciful, green dress with long sleeves, holding her skirts up so she can run at a full tilt. They collide into each others arms, falling in a heap atop thick, summer grass. Alice rubs her muzzle all over Danahlia's smooth, brown neck, desperate to coat herself with as much of the Liguna as she can, while Danahlia wraps arms, legs, and tail about the Tokala, squeezing hard. Alice quickly finds rubs aren't nearly enough and frantically licks her love's chin and cheeks as Danahlia pulls up Alice's blouse so she can run her fingers through the fox girl's fine fur coat while nuzzling her ears.

Alice gets atop the Liguna, rubbing her entire body over her. Danahlia laughs, "Okay, okay, did you really miss me that much?"

Alice's eyes widen at the question. She stops to look down at the grinning lizard girl but rather than answer with words, she kisses her on the lips. Danahlia responds in kind, unable to keep from smiling. They take the time to enjoy one another, their limbs wrapping around and over each other to get every ounce of sensation from the moment. Eventually, they have to breathe.

Danahlia sighs contentedly, "I guess that's a yes."

Alice moans happily, catching her breath as she lies atop her Liguna, rubbing her head into the larger girl's neck. Danahlia pets Alice affectionately for a few precious minutes before she says, "I can't be too long. Let me see Squigs, then I gotta go." Alice frowns, as this was how their secret meetings often went, but leads Danahlia into the forest.

As they walk, Danahlia asks what Alice has been doing, how her father is, and what life is like in Toki village. Alice and her father were currently living in the forest near Toki, among the pixies that dwelt there. The jelly monsters that plagued the forest, and occasionally nearby villages, had multiplied in the absence of the Jellybane. The pixies had cheered her return and welcomed Alice's father and even Squiggles, once they were assured the great dragon was not a threat to them. The wages of a soldier thought long dead were no where near enough to afford a house in Toki village, but that was Robert Dippleblack's goal. For now, the Dippleblacks had begun making a home for themselves deep in the forest in the same ancient ruins Alice and her friends had stayed in years before. With the pixie's guidance, the father and daughter team cleared out infestation after infestation of jellies, taking their valuable pearl like core stones to be traded in for goods they needed and to pay off the debt Alice and her mother had accrued over the years she had been without her father.

They still had a healthy sum to go but with both Dippleblacks raking in core stones, Alice's friend, Ashleigh, and her mother, who ran the trading post in Toki, were able to expand their store and inventory, doing a part to improve the village's long suffering economy. Squiggles wasn't much help in this, as he didn't care for the jellies' taste. And while the dragon's fire could destroy legions of the monsters, in the middle of a dense forest, it was not encouraged that he use it. The pixies did, however, take advantage of the dragon's size, strength, and appetite by luring dangerous creatures to him.

Danahlia is scratching Squiggles over his nose, the dragon's massive head nuzzling her while also gouging up the earth at her feet with his affection. Alice asks from below, picking bits of her shed fur off the Liguna's fancy dress, "So hows married life?"

Without looking down, Danahlia replies, "It's ok. Not really what I had planned but I can't complain."

Knowing Danahlia would have to go soon, Alice asks somberly, "What *did* you have planned?"

Danahlia huffs a little laugh, turning to the fox girl, "Not this," she says gesturing to her fine, green garment. Squiggles nuzzles Danahlia for more pets. She gives him one and then turns to cup Alice's cheeks, "Listen, I gotta go before they start lookin' for me." Danahlia forces a smile, "Need some time to pick all your fluff off my clothes too."

Alice frowns, looking away, but nods.

Danahlia takes the fox girl by the chin and gives her a quick kiss on the lips, "There's this thing I have to go to, it's gonna take a few weeks. I'll send a letter, come back then ok?" Alice's frown deepens and her Liguna assures her, "This isn't forever."

This time Alice forces a smile, "Ok."

Danahlia pats Squiggles' nose once more, bidding them a farewell before running off back toward the estate. Squiggles tries to follow for a moment but Alice stops him. She hated this part. The horrible emptiness in her chest every time

Danahlia left, knowing that this moment marked the longest point before she'd be able to see her again. "A few weeks," she groans to Squiggles

They'd been doing this for some time now, with Alice coming to visit every chance she got. The first months were the worst. Danahlia's wasn't the only arranged marriage after the war. Many of her kin had undergone the same and she and her husband were expected to attend every wedding. It was all a big show of support for the new peace between the nations and it meant Danahlia was away much of the time. But the pair kept believing that after things settled down a bit and everyone got tired of parading the "happy" new couples around, maybe they would have greater opportunity to be with each other. They even made plans for Danahlia to come visit Alice for a while. But even with the weddings finally over, there still just didn't seem to be any time. There was always some noble people's get together, a gala, a ball, some event that would call Danahlia away, which left Alice waiting.

It had to be dark before she and Squiggles could leave the cover of the forest and so Alice uses the time to think, lying atop Squiggles as he wanders around looking for something to eat. At first she thinks of the empty feeling she has and wonders if Danahlia has it to. It was probably worse for her, trapped in her obligation. Danahlia married for her people, not love. Alice knew she wasn't enjoying it but did her best to make the most of it because that's what's expected of her. Alice wasn't an important person in the world. Great things weren't expected of her. She was free. It was a strange thing to think that the more important you are, the less freedom you might have.

Alice was free. And she had a dragon. If she wanted to, she could swoop in with Squiggles and carry Danahlia off with her. That way they could be with each other and have grand adventures all over the world. Alice smiles at the thought. Who could stop them? Then she frowns. Danahlia would. Leaving her marriage might disrupt the peace, maybe even cause the war to start up again. Which would mean people would start fighting and dying again. If that happened, her father would be called away. No, she couldn't do that. Then a new thought enters the Tokala's mind, impossible but entertaining. What if *she* was a noble, and then what if Danahlia could marry *her*. It would still be a union between the warm and cold blooded so the peace could be kept, plus, they would be happy.

Alice lets herself ponder it a bit more, this impossible but entertaining thought, before taking a nap.

Once night comes, Alice flies Squiggles northeast. As Squiggles continues to grow, his flight speed also improves greatly, able to travel farther faster than ever before. She hadn't tried it yet, but Alice is sure that, if he really wanted to, Squiggles could cross all of Arsalia, east to west, in a single day and night. Tonight he wouldn't be flying nearly so far. Alice maneuvers him in the general direction of Borea, a decent sized town near the foot of the Gadara mountains. Alice needed a distraction, and Kaliska's orphanage was a steady source.

Starting out as a hesitant flier, Squiggles now enjoys showing off his top speed for Alice. The Tokala has to keep her body against the dragon's neck to avoid being blown off by the fiercely passing air but cheers the dragon on. Even in summer, at these speeds the air is cold but Alice had grown used to it. She's even come to enjoy it, knowing that the chill over her fur and the loud whistle in her ears meant she was going faster than anyone alive could dream of. She imagines that she's in the midst of a heated battle with dragons, magic, and arrows flying all around. She presses a bare footed heel into the side of Squiggles' thick neck, getting him to bank left, then right, dodging phantom foes.

Within hours, Alice is in familiar skies. From her years living on the Gadara Mountains and trading with the settlements around them, she could recognize the landmarks of the far north even in the dead of night. She has Squiggles set down near a lake hidden in the forest well outside of town. With water nearby and the abundance of the forest, Squiggles would be comfortable for a while. By now he had learned to stay near where they had landed so Alice felt confident he would remain hidden and that she would be able to find him again upon her return. She takes her pack, telling the dragon she will be back in a few days and then makes her way to the settlement.

It's in the afternoon when Alice arrives in Borea. This was a town that existed largely because the local hunters and farmers needed a place to trade goods. It was one of the larger towns Alice knew of, though despite it's size, it wasn't populated enough to be a true city. On most days, the inhabitants were generally out working in the surrounding fields, leaving the town's many streets oddly vacant. By the time Alice is in Kaliska's neighborhood, it's getting close to evening and those she passes are wearily heading home for the day.

As she reaches the Chitali's orphanage, Alice spots Jetta, a jet black Feladine girl, trying to turn away someone who is undoubtedly seeking Kaliska's aid. Kaliska possesses the gift of healing, a magic she shares freely when she can. The deer girl had built a reputation for herself by healing the local sick and injured, of which there was never a shortage. Many would give donations to Kaliska's cause, most amounting to whatever crops they grew, but very occasionally someone Kaliska healed would turn out to be wealthy and give generously in thanks. This allowed Kaliska to buy the modest house the Chitali had turned into her orphanage.

Jetta was one of the first orphans Kaliska and Alice had taken in and had since stayed to help Kaliska in caring for more. Unfortunately, Jetta had remained mute despite Kaliska saying there was nothing preventing her from speaking. This meant the cat girl now only signs and gestures to the young woman asking to see the healer. Alice knew what Jetta was signing but the gestures only seemed to frustrate the woman.

"I'm sorry miss, but she says Kaliska is resting now and you'll have to come back tomorrow," says Alice, walking up to the pair.

The woman turns to her, "Ugh, but my husband collapsed in the fields. He had to be carried to his bed," the woman turns back to Jetta, "Can't Miss Snowtail come for just a short visit?"

Jetta frowns, shakes her head, and mimes sleeping, so Alice tells the woman, "I've known Kaliska for years. She would heal everyone in the whole world if she could, but healing takes a lot out of her. If she stopped for the day, it's because she just can't any more. I'm sure after she gets some sleep, she'll be at it again tomorrow. I'll tell her about your husband."

The woman frets but sees no point in pressing. She thanks the girls and walks off. The moment the woman turns, the Feladine flings herself at Alice and gives her a big hug. Alice returns it, petting the cat girl's fur, "Hey, Jetta." Jetta buries her face in Alice's neck before smiling broadly up at her.

The Feladine leads Alice into the small house where near a dozen children, ranging from very small to mid teens, are sitting about the main room. Their hands are clasped before their mouths as they whisper into them. Then, one by one, the children release their prayers into the air. When they realize Jetta has not returned alone, many voices cheer "Alice!" and "Alice is back!"

After more than a few warm hugs, some voices begin wondering if she brought them anything. Sometimes Alice would bring food, clothes, and, very rarely, even toys. She hadn't had time to visit the market yet, so she reveals her store of core stones, brought all the way from Toki's jelly infested forest. The children grab handfuls of the glowing orbs and play with them in the growing dark. They would have to be traded for more necessary things soon, but for now, Alice enjoys letting the children have some fun with them. Jetta and the other older children have their simple supper prepared shortly and Alice volunteers to take Kaliska's to her.

Alice quietly enters one of the two rooms in the small house to find the deer girl sleeping. This room is kept especially dark so Kaliska can better rest after wearing herself out healing nearly everyday. Alice uses the faint glow from one of her core stones to lightly place Kaliska's meal atop the nightstand beside her bed. She then watches Kaliska sleep, snoring a little, under the glow of the stone. The deer girl is thin, but no more than she usually was, and tall, her slender hooved feet poking out into the air beyond the foot of her bed. Just as Alice is about to begin eating, Kaliska jolts awake.

"Alice?!" the Chitali calls to the room.

Alice lifts her bowl of soup off her lap where some spilled, "Uh, Kali? Yeah it's me."

Kaliska turns to her with urgent eyes, "Alice, where's Twinkles?"

"Who?" Alice asks, "Twinkaleni?"

"Yeah, yeah, Twinkles," Kaliska nods, cupping both hands with fingers splayed over her ears. While Kaliska searches the dark room she asks, "Where is she?"

"Kali, you know I haven't seen Twinkaleni in years," says Alice, handing Kaliska her supper.

"But I just saw her, and you, and Squiggles," Kaliska insists taking her bowl of soup.

"It was just a dream," assures Alice.

"I know," says Kaliska, "Twinkles wanted something."

Alice decides to indulge her, "What?"

"I don't know," Kaliska says frowning, "There was all this rumbling and rocks and stuff, but she wanted something... something from you." Alice raises a brow at the Chitali while she repeats, "Something something, something... something. It's gone. So when did you get in?"

Alice and Kaliska talk for a little bit as they eat. Alice does most of the talking, telling the deer girl about what she and her father had been up to in Toki, how Danahlia is doing, and how Squiggles has been. Kaliska mostly eats, then rests her eyes, and then begins to snore again.

For the next few days, Alice stays with Kaliska and the orphans. Even though most are well behaved, the children must be under constant supervision. They must be fed, clothed, kept clean, healthy, and as entertained as can be managed. Then the house needs to be cared for, with weeds pulled, floors swept, and dishes cleaned. On top of that, visits must be made to the market in order to trade what is had for what is needed. With all the chores, the older children are spread thin and grateful for any help. Plus, someone must always go with Kaliska when she goes out to heal the sick. Though, as her reputation builds, this is less and less of an issue.

Kaliska is not the only healer in Arsalia, but she is among the very few who are not a retainer of wealthy families or charge fees beyond most for their aid. This makes her very popular with the common people and her help highly sought. Because of this, many have begun bringing their ill or injured to her directly rather than waiting for her to come to them. Some even travel from other towns and villages just to see her. Not everyday is so busy, but many days after healing those she can, Kaliska doesn't have the energy to walk back to the house and must be carried in a wheel barrow, cushioned with straw for just such a purpose.

On days that are not terribly busy for Kaliska, she likes to take the children out to the forests and fields surrounding the town too gather medicinal plants and herbs. She teaches the children, in her own unique way, what plants are good for eating and treating ailments. As the children get older, some become well versed in healing with various powders and salves they can make from these plants. This helps lower the burden on Kaliska and will aid them in becoming productive members of society when they feel confident enough to leave the orphanage.

Not all stay until they become old enough to make a go of it on their own however. Some, like Narco, are eventually adopted. Narco was a boy Alice and Kaliska had taken in along with Jetta years before. Under Kaliska and the girl's care, Narco, who had started out very sickly and small, grew into a healthy boy. Ever curious and energetic, he was never meant to stay cooped up at the orphanage and was eventually adopted by a man who had used his wages from the war to buy land for a farm. He felt Narco would be the perfect help to get it off the ground. Though Alice didn't see him this trip, after a good harvest, Narco would often visit to deliver a share of the crop to help the other orphans. But

Narco's was a special case. Those interested in adopting were few and far between, which meant the majority of the children would have to get their start at the orphanage.

After an exhausting stay, Alice decides Squiggles has waited long enough and that it's time to go. Even with all their work, Kaliska's healing, Alice's core stones, and the donations, having so many mouths to feed meant resources were stretched as thin as they could be. The orphanage relied on the supplies bought with Alice's core stones and that meant returning to Toki for more. Finding Squiggles about where she left him, Alice boards the dragon, waits till nightfall, and then heads south back home.

Alice returns to the ruins of what may have once been an impressive fortress or keep, but now was little more than a few crumbling walls and foundations. The one building that still had a serviceable roof was where the Dippleblacks resided. Robert Dippleblack has been hard at work making the old ruin more of a home. Restoring walls, plugging leaks, and getting rid of all the things that had infested the place, plants *and* creatures, took time and effort, but was getting done little by little. Because of their desire to keep Squiggles a secret, the Dippleblacks would decline any offers of help to get them back on their feet. So, for the most part, it was just the two of them.

Supporting themselves wasn't overly difficult, the forest providing in abundance if one knew where to look. The local pixies being their frequent visitors and guides, finding food and water was only a matter of following the tiny, winged fae. Sometimes the pixies would bring their animal friends to deliver various fruits and juices to help encourage the Dippleblacks to hunt the dreaded jellies of the forest. Twinkaleni had told Alice that she believed the jellies were the product of some long gone sorcerer who created the translucent, hemispherical blobs for some unknown reason. As such, they were considered unnatural and could devastate the forest, earning them the pixies' ire. Unfortunately, the diminutive fae folk could do little to stop them. Thus, to preserve their forest, they had few options but to rely on the *taller*, what they called larger people like Alice's kind. But not all taller could be trusted, some even being quite dangerous to the pixies. Having found the Dippleblacks to be an agreeable sort, the tiny fae do what they can to maintain good relations with them.

These good relations could have annoying consequences though. Some mornings would start off with the pixie sisters, Tally and Shae, buzzing around a sleeping Alice, blinking wildly while crying about jellies attacking one of their favored trees. Since the entire forest was important to them, this tended to happen more than the Tokala cared for. Still, jellies meant core stones, so Alice would drag herself from bed to aid her tiny friends.

Continued training with her father was advancing Alice's swordsmanship by the day. This allows for Alice to quickly dispatch jellies wherever they are found. The pixies are ever grateful for this and cheer the fox pair on from a safe height. The jellies have a corrosive touch and must be handled with care. Smaller beings, like the pixies and some of their animal companions, could become absorbed by them if they did not flee. Even as slow as they are, jellies are silent in their approach and readily consume the unwary. This is fairly rare however. Most of a jelly's diet consists of plants, even trees they encounter. Anything caught within the jellies long enough would be dissolved by them, adding to the jellies bulk until they split into two equal but smaller jellies, complete with their own core stones. This, in a dense forest, meant the jellies tended to multiply rapidly if left unattended. This also meant that Alice and her father could gather core stones fairly quickly, and after arriving back on Squiggles, it isn't long before Alice is heading into the village with another cache of cores to trade.

Ashleigh Graysen spots Alice from through the trade post's front window and immediately runs out to greet her.

"Alice," she calls musically. Alice raises a brow. If Ashleigh was this excited, it could only mean one thing. The opossum girl smiles as she curtsies in her simple, blue dress, "Madam, you've a gentleman caller."

Since Alice's return to Toki, she had noticed quite a few young men glancing her way. Many were even veterans of the Blood War looking to settle down to a more peaceful life. Some would come to her directly with requests for her time while others, not knowing where she lived, would leave messages with Ashleigh, since the trading post was a place she frequented. Alice always tried to be polite, knowing it took some courage to profess one's interest in another, telling the hopeful young man that her heart already belonged to someone. Most take her rejection with dignity while others would try to press, making claims of their achievements in the war, the things they could provide for her, and she even heard a few bad poems. If even after rejecting this they continued to pursue, Alice would challenge them to a duel.

There would be a mock battle with sticks pitting Alice against her admirer. This was somewhat part of an agreement Alice had made with her father. Robert Dippleblack had his daughter promise that she would only even consider a suitor worthy if he defeated her in combat. It was a strange promise but one Alice felt she could keep easily enough. Most of the young men would abstain on general principle, but after some taunting, and occasionally a few wacks, Alice could almost always get her suitors to face her. Thus far, they've all left these bouts bruised and disappointed.

Alice sighs at the prospect of refusing the attentions of another hopeful young man and asks disinterestedly, "Who is it this time?"

Ashleigh grins widely, "Guess!" Before Alice can say anything the Didel bursts, "It's someone new! He's not from around here." Ashleigh sidles up to Alice and gives her a few elbows, "He said he has an urgent proposition for you."

This was news, no one had ever come from another town for her before. Then Alice is struck with the thought that it might be an agent sent from the Order of Thermathrogi. Twinkaleni had said it was unlikely but perhaps they had devised a way to track Squiggles using his old teeth or scales left in the Order's academy when she and Alice had made an attempt to free the mages held there. But then why would they be asking for her? As far as she knew, the Order had no idea who she was, unless...

As the realization that in her over three year absence Twinakaleni may have been captured by the Order and forced to divulge information about her accomplices, Alice looks sharply to Ashleigh and asks, "What does he look like? How many were there?"

"Oh, someones interested," Ashleigh grins, lifting a light gray brow, "Well, he's a Lobovan, and... how many? Just the one," Ashleigh giggles, "But he is *handsome.* I think you'll like this one."

One wasn't too bad, but he could have others lurking about or waiting outside of town. Alice demands, "What was he wearing? Was it a red robe? Did he have any rings?"

Ashleigh, seeing Alice's urgency, looks confused, "I, a ring? I don't remember. No red robes. What's the matter?"

Alice crouches to draw a symbol in the dirt, a triangle with three smaller triangles in each corner, and an eye in the hexagon left in the middle. The symbol of the Order of Thermathrogi. She taps the symbol, "Did he have this anywhere on 'im?"

Ashleigh cocks her head at the crude drawing before her feet, "Uh, no. I don't think so. What's that?"

"Remember that order I told you about?"

Ashleigh's eyes widen, "The one that takes the magic children?"

Alice nods, "He might be with 'em. Where is he?"

"He said he'd wait at Hetty's," answers Ashleigh, no longer smiling.

Mrs. Hetty had taken to renting out the empty rooms of her home to travelers while her husband and sons were away at war. Some didn't come back and so Hetty's remained something like an inn.

Alice places a hand on the opossum girl's shoulder, "Ok, I have a big favor to ask."

While exchanging her corestones, the girls discuss a plan to learn more about the visiting stranger. Then the pair head to Hetty's. Once there, Alice sneaks around the side, hopping a fence to take cover behind the wall of Mrs. Hetty's home. Ashleigh approaches the woman directly, tending the garden in front of her house.

"Hi, Mrs. Hetty," Ashleigh calls.

The brown furred, middle aged, Houdain rises at her name, stretching her back, "Why it's the young Ms. Grayson. What brings ya by child?"

"Oh, nothin' much," Ashleigh casually replies, "Momma gave me a lil' break and I wanted to come see your guest. We get so few visitors and all, well, I thought it'd be neighborly."

Mrs. Hetty frowns, taking in a breath to consider before saying, "I suppose it'd be alright. But don't you be a bother. If he wants his peace, you leave 'im be, hear?"

"Oh, I won't be a bother Mrs. Hetty, promise," assures Ashleigh.

Ashleigh is allowed in and Alice sneaks around the side of the house, keeping low. The Tokala makes her way to the window into Mrs. Hetty's living/dining area and spots the Lobovan sitting in a chair reading something. She only gets a glimpse of earth toned fur and a dark, gray blue jerkin before hiding under the window, fox ears perked. She hears Ashleigh enter and greet him but it's muffled. Eventually, Ashleigh opens the window over Alice's head more fully, saying, "There, now isn't that better?"

"Yes, thank you," the wolf man replies curtly in a youthful but strong tone, "Now, I must stress the urgency of my meeting with Alice Dippleblack."

"She'll be around, she'll be around," returns Ashleigh, "Comes in 'bout once a week *and* she's due anytime now. I'll send 'er right over, like I said."

"Please do," says the Lobovan, "If you have not seen her, then may I assume there is something you want of me?"

"Oh, I'm just in between chores and thought you might like some company while you wait. We get so few visitors in these parts," Ashleigh admits.

"Of course, I could use a respite," says the wolf man, then Alice hears the sliding of a chair, "Please, have a seat."

Some chitchat reveals the man to be Sir Lowe Fenris, a name that means nothing to Alice. He claims to be a noble of minor standing from Messena, a territory in central Arsalia, and was sent to Toki on a mission to find Alice Dippleblack. Other than that, he seems hesitant to reveal much about himself or his mission. Every time Ashleigh tries to get more out of him, he easily turns it around, getting the Didel to talk more about herself. As Ashleigh prattles on, she at least manages to keep the Lobovan's attention, allowing Alice to get a better look at him.

He is taller than Ashleigh, even sitting down, two triangular ears listening with interest to the opossum girl. His well kept fur is mostly a deep tan that becomes dark gray as it nears the top of his head. His clothes are more functional than lavish, a leather jerkin over a shirt matching his coat, and dark gray trousers. His tail is thick, full, and sways some with Ashleigh's anecdotes. Unfortunately, this is all Alice can make out from behind. Ashleigh spots her over the wolf man's shoulder and Alice makes a triangle with her hands. Alice then runs a hand over her face when Ashleigh rather tactlessly brings up the Order of Thermathrogi and wonders if Fenris is in some way associated with it. He says he isn't.

After a few more minutes of idle chatter, Ashleigh excuses herself and meets back with Alice. As the pair head to the trading post, they discuss Sir Fenris. Ashleigh is enamored, going on about how handsome and polite he is, while Alice is still unsure if she wants to meet with him.

The two are discussing the mysterious Lobovan when he calls from behind, "Alice? Alice Dippleblack?"

The girls turn to him but say nothing. Sir Fenris approaches, looking to Ashleigh for confirmation but the opossum girl only looks between the two.

"Would you be Alice Dippleblack?" the wolf man tries again.

Still uncertain about the man, though she has to admit, if only to herself, that he is rather handsome, Alice says, "Maybe, who's askin'?"

Fenris looks at her urgently, "I must know for certain."

"She is!" Ashleigh blurts, immediately covering her mouth.

Alice gives Ashleigh a look then replies, "I am. Who're you?"

"Apologies, Ms. Dippleblack," hurries Lowe, "I am Lowe Fenris, vassal to Lady Huld of the Royal Council. I have been sent with a missive to acquire you for a most important mission." Lowe looks to Ashleigh, "If we could have a moment."

Ashleigh whines, "No, come on."

"She's ok," says Alice, not wanting to be left alone with the stranger, "Why do you want *me*?"

"Very well," says Lowe, handing Alice a roll of paper with a red, wax seal, "Alice Dippleblack, Arsalia is under attack by unknown forces. The Royal Council wishes the aid of you and your dragon."

Chapter 3
Call to War

Alice's eyes widen in surprise, "What? Attack? Wh-who says I have a dragon?"

"My lady has instructed me to acquire you both and escort you north to join a force meant to end the threat," explains Lowe, continuing to hold out the letter to Alice until she takes it.

Alice pops the seal on the letter to read, slowly and with a finger on the paper. It says it's from someone named Lady Huld of the Royal Council. She wants Alice *and* Squiggles, she even mentions the dragon by name, to accompany Sir Lowe Fenris to Norwood, a city in the north. There they are to rendezvous with an army under someone named, Lord Nuwald Alvaro. With Alice and her dragon the army will then move into the Gadara Mountains to defeat the enemy led by-

"A titan?!" Alice gasps.

"A titan?" asks Ashleigh, "What about a titan?"

Lowe leans in so others will not overhear, "It is

suspected that a titan leads the enemy invading from the north. Lord Alvaro was part of a force sent to stop it but the enemy proved too great. Many cities have already been attacked, has news not spread?" Alice and Ashleigh look to each other having heard nothing of these attacks, though news would have taken time to reach this far south. Lowe continues, "The attacks have been small, precise hits on major cities. Only Lord Alvaro's encounter with the titan has shown the enemy's true strength. An entire army crushed."

Lowe's words trouble Alice greatly and she attempts to read the rest of her letter. It says that if she accepts, the charges of treason against her will be pardoned. If she succeeds in the mission, she will be offered vassalage under Lady Huld and, upon accepting, be granted the fief of Ardice. If she refuses, she will have the full charge of treason against Arsalia brought upon her for attacking the Order of Thermathrogi's academy at Klepor. She will be executed, her dragon will be seized, and Arsalia may be brought into another prolonged war that will cost many lives, including her father's. The letter says the last with assurance.

Alice tries to take deep breaths but can't and

collapses to her knees.

Ashleigh kneels down beside her, "Alice? What is it?"

Alice had seen a titan once, years ago in the Wildlands. Even from a great distance, the immense creature was an awe-inspiring thing to behold. Now they wanted her to fight one, and if she didn't, they were going to kill her and likely her father. What frightens Alice most is seeing her name, her father's name, and even Squiggles' so clearly written. How could they even know who she was, much less what she had done? She and her friends had taken such care in leaving as little impression on the places they went as they could. That this Lady Huld knew so much made the possibility that Twinkaleni had been captured all the stronger.

Alice's fear begins to turn to anger at the prospect of what might have been done to her Murin friend to make her talk. "Who's Lady Huld?" Alice nearly growls, rising back to her feet, "Where is she?"

Taken aback, Lowe replies, "I, Lady Huld is a member of the Royal Council, and is liege lord of

Messena, where I am from. I could not say where precisely she is now, though it is likely she resides within the capital, Eledon, where the council generally convenes."

For a foolish moment Alice wonders how difficult it would be to ride to the capital, snatch this Lady Huld up in one of Squiggles' claws, and let her dangle a few hundred feet in the air until she told her where Twinkaleni is. *No, that would only make things worse* Alice tells herself. If they did have Twinkaleni, they could use her as a hostage. Plus they could get to Danahlia, and her father, and maybe even Kaliska and the orphans. Alice wasn't even sure if they had Twinkaleni at all. They could have found out about her some other way maybe. There were just too many unknowns.

Alice decides to try, "Do you know a Murin named Twinkaleni Orbear?"

Lowe cocks an eyebrow and then appears to think, "I do not believe so. Will you accompany me then? Time *is* of the essence."

He sounds sincere but it could just be an act. Alice isn't sure what to do.

Lowe then pulls out another rolled letter, "If you refuse, I am to deliver this to your father, Robert Dippleblack."

Alice looks at another wax seal, "What is it?"

"A note of conscription," says Lowe, "The threat of a titan is not to be ignored. If my mission fails, Arsalia's full might will be gathered to face it."

Ashleigh gasps, "No, not another one."

Alice glares at the letter threatening to take her father away to fight in another war. A war against a monster. Alice recalls the trembles sent through the earth as the titan she had once seen walked across the horizon. What could men even do against such a thing?

"Even if I did have a dragon, how am I suppose to fight a titan? Have you ever seen one?" Alice spits.

Lowe stands a little straighter, "I, no, I have not. But we have used dragons to defeat titans in the past. If you have one, yours is the only known to exist in all of Arsalia. It may be all the difference in the battles to come. Make no mistake, the reward for victory is no less than survival. The cost of failure may very well be the fall of the kingdom. Know we have yet to win a single victory over this enemy."

That wasn't very reassuring, though it may have revealed something. They were desperate, this Royal Council. Maybe that's why they felt the need to threaten her so with treason and execution. But what could they really do? She had a dragon. Alice can't help but think if Twinkaleni were here, the clever mage would be able to turn this to her advantage somehow. The only option Alice could see is to accept this quest. Her only *real* choice was what to tell her father.

She had to go. For the sake of everyone she cared for, she had to. Would her father try to stop her? What could he do? Take Alice and leave Arsalia? Fly Squiggles somewhere safe? Could she let him? Flying away might save them, but what about everyone else? If what Lowe says is true, the titan has already destroyed one army full of people, parents and children. How many more would it take? Could it even be done without Squiggles? Could it be done with him? What if her father chooses to come with her, to protect her from the monsters she must face? What if she lost him? He didn't know Squiggles the way she did. What if he fell off? Or was killed in battle? No, he couldn't come. He already fought enough, it was her turn now.

These thoughts pass through her mind is seconds and there is still so much to consider, but Ashleigh is asking in alarm, "What about a titan? They want you to fight one? Is there another war? How can this be?"

Lowe is trying to answer her rapid questions, but Alice interrupts, "Ash, I need you to do one more thing for me."

After explaining what Alice needs Ashleigh to do, she tells Lowe to wait for her on the outskirts of the village while she gets Squiggles from the pixie forest. He wants to follow her but Alice insists he wait, not wanting his presence to make her father suspicious. The Tokala then makes her way back through the forest to begin her mission.

While she walks among the trees she is met by the pixie sisters, Tally and Shae. They are curious as to why she seems so glum, though Alice keeps her true thoughts from them. As usual, they encourage her to face jellies they have seen but Alice refuses, remaining focused on her task. She tells them that she may be gone for a while and that they should seek her father when in need of jelly vanquishing. It is a very long walk to the forest ruins but it does give Alice time to read over the letter some more and think.

She had told Ashleigh of what was to happen and asked her old friend to tell her father the truth of it only when he came looking for her. If Alice's mission took too long, he would undoubtedly find out about the conflict in the north and eventually head there. She desperately wants to keep her father from it for as long as possible, which is why she tells him that she is going to be visiting Danahlia for a time. It was something she did often so it would not be suspicious and would buy her time. She gives him an extra long hug and wishes him good hunting, hoping these would not be her last words to him. Once Alice acquires Squiggles, she heads back to meet with Lowe.

While flying through the night air, Alice wonders if it's fair to take Squiggles on such a dangerous mission. She can't exactly explain the situation and ask him his thoughts, though if his past behavior was any indicator, he would probably be eager to topple a powerful foe. Alice is thinking this when she spots a camp fire on the northeastern outskirts of Toki. Figuring its Lowe and his escorts, she brings Squiggles down to land. If he wanted a dragon, he was going to get one.

The massive reptile sets down heavily just outside the small camp, watching the scrambling of the fearfully shouting men contemptuously. A few take cover behind trees before trembling legs give out while most just cower where they fall. Horses whine and pull at the branches they've been tied to, jerking their heads in an effort to flee.

"Well, we're hear," Alice calls loudly and then begins to dismount.

After a moment, Lowe steps forth, still keeping a cautious distance but at least leaving his tree to meet her. He clearly has trouble looking away from the great reptile as he asks, "Is... is it dangerous?"

Alice tries to keep from grinning as she replies, "Of course he's dangerous. He's a dragon. Isn't that why you people want 'im?"

Lowe's mouth hangs open, "Uh, yes, yes of course."

"He probably won't eat you though, if that's what you mean," says Alice, feeling the dragon looming over her protectively, looking at the tiny man.

"It, uh, obeys your commands?" Lowe asks, he and his men staring in awe.

"He isn't a slave. He's a friend. And his name is Squiggles," Alice replies looking up at the dragon, who has taken an interest in the frightened horses. Alice watches Lowe staring up at Squiggles before reminding, "Hey, you said time was a thing. Let's get goin'."

Lowe has to visibly pull his eyes from the dragon, "Uh, yes, it is. We have a, horse for you..."

Alice interrupts, "Nah, Squigs 'll get us there faster."

Lowe lifts a brow, "You... us?"

Alice nods, turning back to the dragon, "Yup, you're comin' with me."

Lowe instructs his men to meet him at Norwood and is seated behind Alice on Squiggles' back. Squiggles turns his head to look at him as if warning against any offensive behavior and Alice tells him to hold on. She then gives Squiggles a tap of her heels and the great dragon begins to flap his expansive wings. The gust has the small camp fire burning furiously before being snuffed out, causing the men, still staring, to vanish into darkness. Lowe holds on to some of Squiggles' straps, but his legs still meet Alice's. Alice grins as she feels his thighs press more against hers with Squiggles flapping harder and harder.

He says into her ear, needing to be loud over wing beats, "Any advice for a first timer?"

Alice calls back, "Yeah, don't let go!" Just then, Squiggles leaps into the air.

Alice laughs when she hears Lowe yelp, his thighs tight around her own as the dragon begins to ascend. Lowe presses his chest against Alice and she can feel his rapid breaths as Squiggles climbs higher. It gives her a strange sense of satisfaction to feel him so uncomfortable. After reaching cruising altitude, the bumpy ride begins to smooth considerably as Squiggles is able to glide and Alice can feel Lowe begin to relax some.

He says into her ear, "Since I was a boy, it was my dream to ride through the sky on a dragon, like the great warriors of old!"

"I always wanted one too!" Alice calls back, finding it difficult not to get caught up in his excitement.

"However did you find it?" asks Lowe.

"His name is Squiggles! And I found him as an egg!" Alice shouts over the rushing air.

"You fly magnificently, Squiggles!" Lowe shouts aloud.

Alice smiles and gives the dragon a pet along his powerful neck.

Talk turns to the task at hand and Lowe reveals

he has not encountered the enemy they were meant to face. Living in central Arsalia, he was far away from the strikes made on the major northern cities and was not called to join what he calls the coalition force that had faced the titan. He had only heard of the battle before he was tasked with finding Alice and Squiggles.

"You said you were that Huld lady's vassal?" Alice wonders.

"Yes, I am," Lowe answers.

Recalling the note Lowe had given her, Alice asks, "What does that mean?"

Lowe says that a vassal was someone who swore something called fealty to someone else. The Lobovan says this meant he and his family were obligated to do as Lady Huld commands and to support her when the need arises. In exchange for this service, Lady Huld had granted the Fenris family land and title over it. When asked why she was interested, Alice explains what was to be rewarded to her if she succeeds in her mission.

"A most generous offer!" says Lowe, "Should

you accept the mantle of vassal, you would become *Lady* Dippleblack!"

Lady Dippleblack sounds kind of funny but it makes Alice wonder, "Does that mean I'd be a noble?"

Lowe says it would. If she beat this titan, she could become a noblewoman. Alice wonders what this might mean for her and Danahlia. She asks Lowe what a fief and Ardice are. He says a fief is the land on which Ardice, a tiny hamlet surrounded by forest, is on. This would be given to Alice too if she accepts the offer of vassalage. It sounded nice, though these rewards would only be possible if she defeated a titan. And even then, they would place her in the service of Lady Huld, someone who already threatened her life. Alice decides it's best to focus more on her quest than the rewards. They would only be a distraction.

Alice knows in general where Norwood is, having purposely avoided it during her stay in the Gadara Mountains. Lowe hadn't ever been either but it is an obvious sight when they arrive late in the morning. The city is a decent size, but more telling is the large army encampment spanning the countryside just to the north of it. Figuring they are expected, Alice doesn't bothered trying to keep Squiggles' movements hidden and descends enough that Lowe can make out the various standards held before some of the more lavish tents. As they search, the army below riles, calling in alarm and pointing up at them. Squiggles rumbles but Alice keeps him on course.

Lowe points out a red banner with a white tree, a shield on it's trunk, and says it is the standard of Lord Alvaro. A little ways away is a clearing where a bunch of men are standing in neat rows. They panic and flee in all directions when Alice bring Squiggles down to land among them. Quickly, the dragon is surrounded by hundreds of armed men, some angry, some frightened, but most staring open mouthed, all keeping a wary distance. Squiggles bares his teeth at them and Alice must pet him to keep him calm.

After a time, a massive Urock man in heavy looking armor can be seen pushing through the crowd, thundering, "Make way! Make way you fools!"

Parting the sea of men, the Urock breaks free

into the large empty circle around Squiggles. Trailing behind him are a youngish Lobovan, an older looking Murin, and a middle aged Lutarin, all wearing very fancy clothes.

Lowe leans into Alice, "Lords Danior, Alvaro, and Winchell. The Murin is Alvaro. We are meant to report to him. I know you are not accustomed to such meetings. As such, I strongly advise you to use their titles when addressing them. Interactions with such people always go much smoother if proper respect is shown."

Alice glances back at Lowe who gives her a pleading look. Squiggles glares at the fancily clothed men looking warily back at him. Alice pets Squiggles and calls in a soothing voice that they are ok. He looks back at her questioningly but Alice insists. The dragon then crouches to let his passengers off. The lords are hesitant to approach any further so Alice and Lowe go to them.

The Urock grumbles, "Don't like the way your beast is lookin' at the lords."

A long time ago, Alice might have been made wary of such an imposing man, but years of rigorous training has given her a confidence that tells her big men are slow and tire quickly. Ones in armor even more so. She looks back at Squiggles, eyeing the bear man, and says, "He's hungry. Try not to look so much like something he'd want to eat."

Lowe quickly brushes past her, knocking her slightly with his elbow, before kneeling in front of the fancy men, "My Lords, may I present to you, Alice Dippleblack and her mighty Gullveigaryan."

The wolf and otter lords, still marveling at Squiggles, let Lord Alvaro approach alone. He says in a pleased but small voice, "It is most excellent to see your mission was a success, Sir Fenris. Your Lady will be informed of your prompt delivery. Well done."

Lowe is saying, "You honor me, my Lord," though Alvaro is already making his way to Alice.

The mouse lord comes up to about Alice's chest in height. Over nearly white fur, he wears what Alice guesses are leather garments, mostly red, embroidered with intricate gold patterns that glimmer with his movements. On his chest is the same tree from his standard. Squiggles takes interest in the Murin's approach, craning his neck to bring his massive head closer. Seeing this, the Murin freezes, large green eyes upon the dragon looming several stories over him. All around men call nervously to the mouse lord.

"It's ok, he's just being protective. Don't make any sudden movements and he won't get upset," announces Alice, then to Alvaro, she quickly adds, "My Lord."

"Uh, of course," says Alvaro, glancing to Alice and back at Squiggles before slowly resuming his approach, "Alice Dippleblack, I am Nuwald Alvaro, Lord of Raingeir, and Commander of the secondary coalition force. It is truly a shame our meeting had to be under such circumstances but Arsalia is in need of your aid. As the only dragon rider in all the kingdom, we must place a terrible burden upon you and your dragon. I take that your being here now means you accept?"

Alice's brow furrows and after a deep breath she replies, "I don't have much choice."

"Nor do we all," Lord Alvaro gestures to all the men assembled, "But this titan and it's minions *must* be stopped."

"Have you seen it then? The titan?" asks Alice, then remembers to add, "My Lord."

"I have, though I am aware some doubt my word. I along with Lord Danior were part of the first army sent to face the northern threat. A battle that cost us many good men, including our former commander, Lord Argus Blackburn." Alice is about to say she's sorry but Alvaro continues, "The enemy proved that day to be far more clever than we imagined. We thought they merely brutes, strong if mindless, but they set a trap for us. We must not make the same mistake again."

Alice asks, "How big was the titan? The one I saw was like a living mountain. Even with Squiggles, I don't know what you expect me to do against that."

The two other lords have joined them and the Lutarin asks in disbelief, "You've seen a titan, Lady Dippleblack?"

"Yeah, once, in the Wildlands," says Alice.

The lords look to each other before the

Lobovan asks irritated, "You saw the titan and reported it to no one?"

"It was years ago, and who would I report it to? We were in the Wildlands," Alice shoots back.

"Insolent girl, knowing the enemy we faced would have saved many lives!" the Lobovan snarls.

"Lord Danior! You make many presumptions," interjects Alvaro.

The Lutarin adds more calmly, "Indeed. Who knows what the young lady saw. Presuming it was a titan, could it even be the one we face?"

"I did see a titan," Alice insists, "It was tall as a mountain, and even though we were far away, me and my friends could feel it shake the ground with each step!"

Squiggles lowers his head over Alice and snorts, showing his displeasure at the raised voices.

"Perhaps we could, discuss matters further in my quarters, over some refreshment," suggests Alvaro. The other lords agree so Alice does too.

Squiggles rumbles and Alice assures him she will be back soon. Alvaro wonders, "Will your dragon be... well, my lady?"

Alice looks back at Squiggles. Turning to watch her go, his tail sweeps into several tents as men retreat from it. "Uh, yeah, but he could probably eat and use some water. He likes meat, and rocks."

Alvaro looks to the heavily armored Urock man beside him, "Water, meat and, um, rocks for the dragon." The bear man puts a fist over his heart and bows before breaking away to yell orders to some of the soldiers.

As men are slowly put back to their duties, the Lobovan lord grandly announces, "We have a dragon!" Men cheer loudly as he adds, "Our enemy will fall before Arsalia's might!"

"I do hope Lord Danior's enthusiasm is not premature," Alvaro says to Alice.

"Lowe isn't coming?" Alice wonders, seeing the Lobovan disappear into the crowd of soldiers.

The Murin lord looks to Alice, "Sir Fenris? His

mission is done for now. He will rejoin the ranks and prepare for the battles to come. As I believe we all must."

Alice is led into a large tent with a round table within it. She and the three lords are seated, a boy in his teens even pulling her seat out for her. He then pours some deep red liquid into goblets and sets one before each lord and her. Alice is pretty thirsty and sniffs curiously at her cup. It smells strong but somewhat fruity. The others seem to be enjoying it so Alice takes a sip. It's terribly bitter and Alice sets the goblet down, making a face. This seems to amuse the others and Alvaro tells the boy to bring her water.

Some food is brought in the form of small biscuits, which a hungry Alice is delighted to find are stuffed with thick meat sauces the likes of which she had never had. As she partakes generously of these, the Lords ask her questions, mostly about Squiggles. They are very interested in hearing how Alice had acquired him. Alice keeps her answers vague, saying she found him alone as an egg in a cave on a mountain while she was traveling. Alice wishes to keep the location of the dragon nest a secret, feeling for some reason that if it became common knowledge, no other dragons would risk laying there again. As they talk, more men arrive. They are greeted as Lord this or that and take seats.

Many seem surprised that the one who brought the great dragon amidst their camp is a young woman, though some comments are made about some of the greatest of Arsalia's dragon champions having been women. They greet her as Lady Dippleblack and most are polite about it. Alice is asked a great many times about where she found Squiggles, and again and again she answers in the same vague manner. She is content to let them think of her as some ignorant peasant girl, knowing they need her a lot more than she needs them. As the table begins to fill, talk turns to the conflict at hand. It's a bit uncomfortable to be surrounded by so many men in such a confined space but Alice does her best to listen.

Alvaro hushes the gathering, small among his counterparts, "My Lords and Lady, I do not know what you have heard of the conflict but I thank you for your attendance."

A deeply voiced, and not overly polite, Bovidan says, "Heard someone was invadin' from the north, with a titan no less." Some of the others rumble their agreement.

"It is true," says the young Lobovan, Lord Danior, "Lord Alvaro and I have faced it." Another rumble, this one questioning and unbelieving.

One man claims, "There hasn't been a titan in Arsalia in hundreds of years."

Cutting off similar comments, Alvaro says loudly, "Yes, my Lords, but there *have* been titans in the past, and we believe there is one threatening us now. And it is not alone."

"What? *More* than one titan?" asks another man.

Alvaro again raises his voice to cut off another wave of talk, "We do not know. We underestimated the enemy once, and for it, lost Lord Blackburn and nearly our entire force."

"What else do we face then?" asks a calmer voice from a Feladine.

"From what we have seen, stone warriors we

are told are called golems make up the bulk of the enemy's numbers," answers Alvaro.

The gathered lords talk among themselves and the Bovidan bellows, "Stone men? Titans? Sounds like children's tales. Me and my men didn't come all this way to fight you northmen's fantasies."

He gets some agreement from the others but Lord Danior counters, "It's true! We fought them. Massive men made of stone. They killed many!"

The Bovidan tosses back, "Somethin' killed Blackburn and a few of your men, but I doubt it was some story book monsters."

The Lobovan is about to snarl something back but Alvaro raises his small pink hands, "Lord Danior, Lord Kyland, I believe that will do."

"It is a bit difficult to believe," says the Feladin, "After all, the Gadara Mountains are home to no such creatures, and beyond are the Wildlands. In all of Arsalia's history, there has never been mention of people living there. Even if there were, why would they attack? Why now?"

More agree to this, but Lord Alvaro points out, "The Wildlands remain largely unknown to us. And thus far, of the northern invaders, none have been people, warm or cold blooded. All we have seen are the stone golems and their titan."

Alice had kept to herself during the talks thus far, but a thought occurs to her, "What if they're not golems? What if they're elementals?" All the men turn to her and she immediately shrinks into her seat, regretting saying anything.

Alvaro asks, "Elementals, Lady Dippleblack?"

With so many eyes upon her, Alice feels compelled to explain, "Uh, yeah. Golems are made by mages. Mages have to be nearby to control them. If you haven't seen any people, then how could they be golems?" Most look at her blankly so she continues, "Elementals, though, they don't need mages. They're natural, like ferals, and can move on their own."

Some of the men look to Alvaro though the Feladine asks Alice, "How do you know of such things, my lady?"

"Uh, I had a friend who, knew a lot about magical things," replies Alice, not wanting to reveal too much.

"What good does that do us? Golems? Elementals? All stories," grumbles the Bovidan, Lord Kyland.

Another makes a disgusted noise at the bull man, "Don't you see what she's sayin'? If it were golems up in those mountains, all we'd have to do is kill the mage workin' 'em. But if they're elementals..."

The Feladine asks the group, "I'm afraid I've not kept up on such lore. How *does* one defeat an elemental?"

When no one is forthcoming, Alice offers, "Squiggles, my dragon, he can. His fire burns them, he's done it before.

"Burn stone?" Kyland grumbles, "I'd like to see that."

Before Alvaro can intervene Alice counters, "It's not the stone he burns. Elementals are formed by magic, natural magic. It's that he burns."

"We have beaten the smaller ones as well," adds Danior, "It takes a great deal, but men can fell these creatures too. It is the titan that poses the greatest threat."

"If I recall my history, my Lords," says an older Didel, "It took many dragon riders to defeat even a single titan. Can it be done with only one?"

The gathered lords murmur among themselves until Alvaro looks to Alice, "Lady Dippleblack, I know it is a terrible burden to place upon you, but do you believe you and your dragon will be able to face a titan? Despite our efforts, I believe you would be alone in this task."

The other lords quiet to listen and Alice considers for a moment, recalling the sheer size of the titan she had once seen. The prospect of facing one in battle seems insane but what choice did she have? Alice takes a breath, "I don't know if or how a titan can be beaten. I only heard stories about them being defeated by dragon riders when I was small. But if it means saving Arsalia, then, I'll at least try."

"Well said," says the Feladine. Then to the others, "What more can we ask of ourselves or anyone?"

"If it's true, and this girl will face a titan for Arsalia," Kyland rumbles, "then we'd all be cowards not to ourselves!"

The other lords agree to this and discussion turns to strategy.

Chapter 4
Battle

While amassing a new army, Alvaro informs the other Lords that he has chosen to keep the bulk of his troops in Norwood, while dispatching detachments to garrison northern cities and larger towns. Norwood has yet been struck by one of the strange raids that have plagued surrounding cities for the last many months. He believes this makes it a likely target. Though if he is wrong, it's central position should allow for reinforcements to be sent where they are needed while the garrisons in each city hold off the enemy. The Murin commander thinks that now that the raiders have revealed their true strength and even struck down an entire army with it, a large scale attack will come to capitalize on Arsalia's weakness.

As more men arrive by the day to join the ranks, all those already assembled end up waiting for news of the predicted attack. Ornivian scouts have been sent into the mountains to try to find the enemy but thus far, of those that returned, none have found anything resembling an army or titan. Scouts on foot have also been sent but the mountain's rocky terrain means they are slow to report if they manage to at all. Alice learns these things in various meetings Alvaro holds as his army assembles. Even given her own personal quarters, Alice finds she doesn't care much for the crowded military camp and the many stares she draws. Under the conditions that she report in frequently and drag Sir Lowe Fenris around, Alice is freed to fly Squiggles to nearby forests.

She doesn't mind the Lobovan's company. After all, he seems endlessly interested in hearing about her life, so different from his own. He grew up the son of a nobleman, but despite having land and title, his family is not particularly rich. Though he admits he's never had to wonder when his next meal might come like Alice had when she was younger. He claims his life seems particularly boring compared to Alice's many adventures, sighting that while she was feeding herself by slaying monsters, he was occupied with learning all about Arsalia's various houses and their relations. While she was making friends with pixies, he was learning proper horsemanship. He also says he was taught how to wield a sword from his father as Alice was, so naturally, the Tokala must test him, if only to pass the time.

It takes some coaxing, and a few insults, but he eventually does agree to it. Squiggles referees as the two square off.

"My lady, are you sure this is entirely necessary?" asks Lowe, looking at the stick in his hand.

"It is if you plan on defendin' your daddy's honor," Alice shoots back, dancing around to the Lobovan's side.

Lowe sighs, "I do not wish you harm, my lady."

"That's fine," Alice grins, just before bringing her own stick in a high arc aimed at the wolf noble's head.

In a blur of motion, he turns to Alice, catching her stick with his own. Alice's grin widens.
The fox maiden dances around the Lobovan some more, testing his defenses. She broadcasts her blows, watching his reactions to them. He keeps her in view and repels her stick with well placed blocks, though he doesn't strike back. He hasn't gotten there yet. She knows, like most men, he needs to be riled up before he takes her seriously. Alice steadily

increases the speed of her attacks, forcing Lowe to work to keep up with her. She gives him a fairly steady pattern, letting him get comfortable. As he attempts to block another blow, Alice adjusts the attack, whacking Lowe's fingers.

Lowe grunts in surprise and pain.

Alice gives him some space before taunting, "Oh, did that hurt? Just so you're not caught off guard again, the next ones gonna hurt even more." Lowe flexes his aching fingers and gives Alice a look, but then he just smiles and raises his stick to her. *Good, almost there.*

Alice moves in again. Lowe keeps mostly to a stubborn defense, but does attempt a clumsy strike when Alice leaves herself open to it. She dodges under it and gives his knee a solid knock. He staggers before trying for another attack but Alice is already out of range.

"Gettin' there," Alice muses aloud.

Lowe gives her a half smile and pursues. He attacks a bit more but is obviously holding back. After a few more strikes, he still isn't performing to

Alice's expectation and she is getting bored. She decides enough is enough and strikes him rather hard atop the head. He drops to one knee, feeling the spot between his ears, his stick on the ground.

He sees Alice frowning at him and admits, "My lady, your ability is well beyond my own, well struck."

Alice exhales through her nose and says darkly, "You're a coward."

"Now, my lady, that is uncalled for," he says, still rubbing his head, "I fought and lost, let me keep some dignity."

Alice narrows her eyes and raises her stick in both hands, bringing it down with all her strength atop the man's head. He raises his arms in defense, but just before she lands the blow she stops, muttering, "You're afraid."

Lowe looks at her from around his upraised arms as Alice continues, "You're afraid that even if you fight me with everything you have, I'll still beat you. You don't want me to embarrass you, so you're just gonna give up. You're a coward."

"That is *quite* enough, Lady Dippleblack," growls Lowe.

Getting upset now, Alice brandishes her stick, "I challenged you so we could learn from each other and become better swordsmen. I really don't like that you'd deny me the chance to improve because you're afraid of gettin' embarrassed. We might be fightin' in a war soon and not being the best I can might get me killed. I don't plan to die in your war just because you're a coward."

Lowe tries to speak but Alice cuts him off, glancing to where the pair had placed their real weapons, "You know what? I'm gonna knock you out. Then, I'm gonna shave off all that well groomed fur o' yours."

Lowe protests, "Lady Dippleblack!"

"Then," Alice glares back at Lowe, cutting him off again, "I'm gonna drop you off in the middle o' camp naked so the whole army can see Sir Lowe Fenris, the pink bellied coward."

"You're mad!" gasps Lowe, "Lady Dippleblack,

you-"

"I'm not a lady," shoots, Alice raising her stick, "I wasn't born with a fancy *title*!" She strikes Lowe's defending arms hard. "My family never had *land*!" She hits him again, aiming for his head, and then again when she snarls, "I had to earn everything I *have*!"

Lowe endures the bruising blows, trying to catch Alice's battering stick. Failing, he picks his own back up, yelling, "Stop!" swinging wildly but missing.

He does get Alice to back away, giving him a moment to rise to his feet. He stands with the stick before him, "You will cease this at once!"

Finally Alice thinks, but says aloud, "Will I?" before attacking again.

At last, Lowe's anger and pain begin to reveal his true skill. He's aggressive and quick, first trying to take Alice's stick away, and then lashing out at her when she doesn't let him. Once his initial rage settles, he begins to fight more earnestly. He even catches Alice with a punch to the cheek, when he forces her to block. He immediately recoils to apologize but this only leaves him open to a round house kick Alice plants on the side of his head.

Even with a throbbing cheek, Alice has him down to one knee again and he glares at her as she taunts, "Save your apologies for when you lose."

Lowe sweeps his stick up at her. Alice knows she's out of range and doesn't dodge, which allows the maneuver to fling dirt into her face. Alice turns away to avoid it and gets a sharp whack on her back. She yelps and staggers away, hearing Lowe behind her, "So certain I will?"

Pain and burning embarrassment fueling her, Alice launches into a series of strikes that Lowe struggles to repel. Even enduring a few hits, he grins and Alice knows she's made a mistake. She let him get her angry. Her father would be disappointed if he saw this.

Anytime they had sparred and Alice got angry her father would make them stop. That tended to make Alice even angrier, but when she attempted to lash out, he would simply knock her weapon away and hold her down. He'd tell her that getting angry might give you strength but it also made you reckless, and recklessness gets you and others killed. It is the mark of a true warrior to know when to use anger and when to conserve it.

Alice tries to back away and give herself a moment to breathe but Lowe keeps on the pressure. He's stronger than she by a fair margin, but that was something Alice was used to. After blocking a few blows, Alice evades low to his left, delivering a swift pommel strike to the side of his knee. He barks in pain, Alice's stick having a jagged bottom. Before she can pass him though, Lowe hammers his fist painfully on her back. Alice takes it and manages to get some distance as Lowe looks at the hole in his pants. A bit of his fur pokes out, stained red with his blood.

"Not bad, for a girl," he mocks, turning to face her.

Alice ignores her pain, putting on a grin, "Maybe I'll take your manhood along with your fur. That way, people can say the same about you."

Lowe grins back, "You are welcome to try."

As the pair continue their bout, Lowe wonders,

"If I lose, you get my fur–"

"And manhood," Alice adds.

"And manhood," Lowe corrects himself, "What is it *I* get if *you* lose?"

Alice sweeps to Lowe's side, connecting with his shin, "You get to keep 'em. Thought that was obvious."

Lowe manages to block Alice's next strike, "That's hardly fair. If you lose, you should give something up as well."

"You're bigger *and* stronger than me," Alice says ducking under a blow and redirecting another, "How is this fair?"

"As I recall, you challenged me, *my lady*," he says the honorary sarcastically. When they lock sticks, he adds, "I believe, when I beat you, I shall have a kiss."

Alice breaks the lock and swings at Lowe's sword hand, forcing him back, "Fine, kiss yourself all you want."

Lowe cocks a brow, "I mean from you."

"Oh, forgive me, *Sir* Fenris, my *lord*, my *liege*" Alice says with a bow, in her best lowly peasant voice, "But all I have to offer are *beatings*!"

Lowe deflects her lunge, giving her a tisk tisk tisk, "Ladies curtsy."

"I'm no lady!" shouts Alice, lunging again and only narrowly missing Lowe's face.

The two fight until both are breathing raggedly, their movements slowed to a crawl. Alice sags, far too stubborn to give up, and Lowe huffs, "You look tired, my lady. Perhaps you should sit down."

"You're one, to talk," mocks Alice, pointing out the Lobovan's own shaky stance.

"You did stab, my knee," Lowe tosses back.

Alice smirks, "Yeah, you should be, more careful, or it might happen, again."

"I doubt it," growls Lowe as he charges.

Seeing this, Alice hurls herself at Lowe, the last of her strength all that keeps her standing. Using more her weight then any energy she has left, she strikes over hand. He slashes high. Their sticks clash, crack, and break. The two knock heads, bouncing off of each other before falling back onto their rears.

Lowe rubs his forehead, looking down at his broken stick, "It seems, I'll be keeping, my manhood, then."

Alice, doing the same, tosses what's left of her stick at him. It bounces off his leg and she grumbles breathlessly, "For now."

Squiggles yawns disinterestedly, having grown used to seeing Alice spar.

The two make a habit of their duels, neither ever admitting to a loss, while the Arsalian army is left waiting to counter an attack that has yet to come. Alice finds herself thinking that Lowe is a decent enough opponent and a good distraction from the nervous fear wiggling around her gut about eventually facing a titan. When not honing their skills on each other, the Tokala and Lobovan fly about on Squiggles, making sure the dragon is fit for duty at a moment's notice. Plus it's fun. Lowe gets especially uncomfortable when Alice has Squiggles do sharp turns and rolls, so she does them often. She especially likes the way he grabs hold of her and makes nervous little noises he tries desperately to contain when they're upside down. He has little choice but to endure it, as he was assigned to watch over her. Then, when they land and he's upset about the whole thing, Alice explains that it's all for his benefit. She says that if he were to accompany her into battle, as he is meant to, and Squiggles needed to make swift maneuvers that the brave Sir Lowe Fenris was unprepared for, then the poor knight would surely fall to his death. Alice is sure to stress what a terrible, *grievous* loss that would be, not only to her, but to the whole of Arsalia. So she tells him that he needs to get in as much practice as he can.

Alice also finds that among the Ornivians serving the army is a Wakuwai from the Cloudstalker tribe. She surprises the young hawk man by speaking in his people's language. His name is Canowi and says he also served in the Blood War, mostly as a message carrier, but was drafted into this new conflict primarily as a scout. Able to fly with their massive wings, Ornivians could travel faster and see farther than anyone stuck on the ground, giving them high value in the army. He expresses concern over other Ornivians that have been sent to find the current enemy but have yet to return. The Gadara Mountains are covered with especially tall trees that grow thick in most places. This would force the airborne scouts to venture low to the ground in order to find enemies hiding under the forest canopy. Doing so would have made them vulnerable and, the young scout states, is likely the reason so many have not come back.

The wait goes on for several weeks with mounting pressure from the gathered lords pushing Alvaro to act. Already dubious over the possibility that a titan could not only be attacking Arsalia but leading an army, many question Alvaro's claims. The Murin lord stresses the need for patients, as they know little of their enemy's whereabouts as well as their total troop strength. The men grow weary of hearing Alvaro's cautioning against walking into another trap and become more restless by the day. This new army is considerably larger than the first and momentum builds behind the idea that such a force could sweep the entirety of the Gadara

Mountains with ease. Braver than Alice feels they should be, a few soldiers even spread word that some of the other lords plan to take command from the cowering Alvaro and move on the mountains without him. Some even talk of simply leaving. His army arguing and threatening to fall apart, Alvaro finally calls for a march to the foot of the mountains.

A marching army is a slow thing. Squiggles could fly to the mountains within hours easily, but Alvaro insists Alice stay with the main force, frequently flying over it to help boost morale. The army is eventually split into several large brigades, each sent to search a particular section of the massive mountain range. Even so, they will only be able to cover a small portion at a time, but Alvaro feels it will be the safest way to proceed while keeping their strength high. The areas to be searched are those closest to raided cities as well as areas with a high loss rate of scouts. Alvaro feels the greater loss of scouts means the enemy is likely hiding nearby. Alice is kept with the Murin commander's central group.

Once they reach the edge of the vast forest that grows upon the Gadara Mountains' foot to nearly it's many craggy peaks, the brigades split once more, sending battalions of soldiers up more manageable paths. The bulk of the army remains at the foot of the mountains to reinforce it's smaller detachments as needed. The goal of the smaller formations was to pose a target large enough to be a threat but small enough to make the enemy overconfident in attacking it. Once engaged, the smaller detachments were to retreat, luring their pursuers to the waiting brigades.

Squiggles seems oblivious to the situation, even excited to be back among the mountains where he and Alice had lived for several of his younger years. The army is quite a bit west from where Alice and her friends had stayed but she too feels some comfort in being in the mountains again despite the threat. Beyond the large groups of men, the Gadara Mountains look as peaceful and full of life as they ever had. It's difficult for Alice to believe that a war was being fought here. With her knowledge of the range, she wants to move ahead with the scouts but Alvaro feels she is too valuable to risk, which means more waiting.

After several days of fruitless searching, Alvaro is about to call another march so his brigades can catch up to the smaller battalions further up the mountains when word of attack comes. Alice is flying over the army with Squiggles and Lowe when she spots an Ornivian racing toward them. It's Canowi, the young Cloudstalker. He dives for Alvaro in the center of the formation below. Alice takes Squiggles lower and after a moment Canowi flies up to join her. He frantically reports that a western battalion is under attack and Alvaro wants Alice to aid them immediately. After a few breaths to process, Alice has Squiggles follow Canowi to the battle.

Flying well over the massive Zalonya trees that grow all over the mountains, it only takes a few minutes to reach the embattled battalion. Alice can instantly see they're in a bad spot. The soldiers had tried to scale the side of a mountain by traveling up a shallow valley. There are cliffs on either side of them, keeping them tightly packed as dust clouds form thick trails from further up their path. Before each bellowing dust trail, Alice can make out massive boulders rolling into and over the men. Even from high in the air, she can hear them screaming.

Lowe calls to her from behind, "We must aid them!"

Alice knows but isn't sure how. Her first instinct is to get Squiggles to stop some of the boulders but Canowi takes her attention. He directs her up the incline to where several large, gray figures are busy pushing over the deadly boulders onto the Arsalians. Alice heads for them with all haste, letting her fear become anger. As she nears, she finds the figures appear to be men though several times larger than even the biggest Urock she had ever seen. They shove a neat row of boulders over, setting them to roll down atop the warm blooded soldiers with a strange efficiency that makes the process look planned. They are so focused on their work that they don't even notice the dragon falling upon them until Alice shouts, "INFERMIOUS!"

Squiggles lets out a vicious roar that makes the air around Alice feel like it vibrates. With it, he pours fourth a massive column of fire down on the strange men. Alice has Squiggle pull up from his attack to avoid a possible counter. Both she and Lowe look back to see the men are still working. They and the ground around them are set ablaze, greenish flames replacing the orange Squiggles had bathed them in but they just keep pushing over more boulders.

Shocked, Alice brings Squiggles around for another pass, but as she does, the strange men begin to crumble and collapse. They fall mid motion into heaps of what look like rocks making no sounds of pain at all.

"What monsters are these?" wonders Lowe.

"They're elementals," says Alice, getting Squiggles to hover, "I guess Alvaro was right." They didn't look like the elemental Alice and Squiggles had once faced, but that green fire and the way they crumbled under it has Alice sure. They aren't men at all but beings of magic. As she is looking over them, movement catches her eye and she spots a few more retreating for the safety of the trees. Alice has Squiggles give chase, but they're among the dense forest before he can get them in range.

"You have beaten them back, my lady!" announces Lowe, giving Alice's shoulder a squeeze, "The first victory of what I'm sure will be many!"

Alice feels the tightness in her gut weaken considerably at this and she flies Squiggles back to the battalion. The soldiers cheer her arrival and she has Squiggles help them remove some of the boulders from their comrades. Despite routing the elementals, many men were killed, including the officer in charge. Even more were wounded. Some had limbs crushed by the boulders while others were trampled in the panic to flee from their path. Their cries of pain and for help are terrible. The healers of the army were kept with the brigades meaning they had no skilled hands among the soldiers to give aid. Alice isn't much of a healer, but spending time with Kaliska has taught her a few things about dressing wounds.

She tries to dismount Squiggles but Lowe stops her, "My lady, we should keep aloft."

Alice looks back at him in surprise, "But they need help."

"Other battalions may come under attack. Without you to support them, many more will perish," reasons Lowe. Alice considers his words and the Lobovan puts a gloved hand on her shoulder, "These are soldiers. Let them do soldiers' work. You are a dragon rider. Your place is in the sky."

Alice takes one more look around at the men gathering their wounded and figures Lowe is right.

This battle is over but there will likely be more. She has Squiggles return to the air but before he can even reach a comfortable height, another Ornivian flies down to meet her. This one isn't Wakuwai but resembles more a crane with his long narrow beak and slender limbs. He lands atop Squiggles behind Alice and Lowe, before gasping of another attack on a battalion that Alvaro wishes her to reinforce. Alice encourages Squiggles on, following the crane man's direction.

As they fly back east, Alice can see a few other battalions seem to have been hit as well. Large boulders sit among recovering groups of soldiers, dust still settling over some, though no actual fighting seems to be taking place.

"They were waiting for us," states Lowe, "They know the high ground gives them an advantage."

Alice only nods, thinking back to what little she knew of elementals. The one she had faced years ago was strangely shaped, asymmetrical and almost crab like with all it's limbs. It seemed mindless in it's anger, lashing out without being provoked, though it did show some level of intelligence in hurling stones when it couldn't physically attack. These new ones were different, not only in appearance but in tactical thinking. They seemed to be laying traps, though it was possible that they merely defended their home when confronted by strangers. Alice is wondering if her and Squiggles' defeat of the first elemental has anything to do with all those attacking now. She is thinking that maybe they are not mindless at all. That maybe an entire society of them lived in the mountains and only took time to unify against the ones who had killed one of their own. The Ornivian, still aboard Squiggles, cuts short the thought. He points and then takes flight to his battalion scattered below.

They were hit hard with boulders. Not trapped in a valley like the first group, they managed to spread themselves out to help mitigate casualties. Even so, it's clear that this was a much larger attack than the others. Alice searches the top of the incline the soldiers had taken but sees no sign of any elementals. The attack was already over. Under Lowe's insistence, Alice continues to have Squiggles fly about but it seems the fighting is done for the day. As evening comes, Alice is asked to report back to Lord Alvaro.

The Arsalians suffered many casualties during

the first day of fighting, but these are only a negligibly small portion of the Warm Blood's forces. The Murin commander is pleased to hear of Alice's defeat of several elementals, the only ones so far, and has word spread throughout the army of their dragon rider already contributing greatly to the war effort. There have been no sightings of the titan supposedly leading these elementals but considering their greater effort in defending the eastern front, Alvaro is confident that the rock people's main camp is there. Wishing to strike at the heart of the enemy before more traps can weaken his forces, Alvaro has most of the army march to reinforce the brigades in the east while leaving some to protect their rear. Now knowing they face a dangerous foe, the men seem more unified and accepting of their diminutive commander's orders.

After a night's rest, Alice and Lowe are tasked with flying ahead to aid the far eastern front while the main force marches to join it. Alvaro says it will take several days to regroup and make his way there. He asks that Alice ensure the eastern brigades are able to hold until then. Alice agrees to this and finds herself glad she isn't in a command position. It looked very difficult to manage the lives of so many. Breakfast the next day is rushed when word reaches that the east is under attack once more.

As Lowe and Alice scramble to prepare, the Lobovan tries to get Alice to wear the thick leather armor that had been in the works since Norwood. Even made specifically for Alice's slender body, it still felt heavy and restricting. Lowe was wearing plate mail and looked every part the brave knight with his heavy kite shield and longsword. She wonders why he bothers, seeing as he'll be flying on Squiggles and not facing the enemy directly. He gives her some line about a knight having to protect his lady and says it would boost the men's morale if they looked the part of real dragon riders. He continues to press for her to wear her own armor and she eventually concedes to wearing the helm, chest piece, greaves, and bracers. Dyed deep red, nearly as dark as Squiggles' scales, they did look rather wags. Alice hurries into them, Lowe helping to tie off bits for a snug, secure fit and the pair take off.

Under the guidance of another Ornivian, Alice hurries Squiggles on. Her heart beats quickly at the prospect of another battle, a mix of adrenaline and fear running through her. Her lateness to the last ones weigh on her, knowing if she doesn't arrive in time all she will end up doing is looking down at all the casualties. Squiggles flies quickly, perhaps feeling Alice's unease and sense of urgency. It doesn't take long to find the eastern battalions, particularly because of all the smoke.

At first, Alice thinks it must just be the many camp fires of a large number of soldiers, but as they get closer, the smoke trails prove far too thick. The Ornivian recounts that in the early morning, his battalion was awoken by flames, presumably the elementals having rolled massive, burning logs upon them as they slept. Not wanting to lose the ground they had sacrificed the day before to gain, the soldiers had made camp above where the elementals had been waiting to roll boulders upon them. It seems the elementals made them pay for it. Alice urges Squiggles on faster as they near, hearing a great deal of activity through the gray haze.

A battle rages below amidst fire and smoke. The smoke is pluming from what Alice immediately knows are the gargantuan trunks of the local Zalonya trees. Somehow the elementals have cut the sky scraping trees down and set them ablaze before rolling them over the Arsalian soldiers. Many have caught on rocks and each other to create an impenetrable wall of flame, preventing the soldiers from retreating down to the safety of the larger brigade trying to reinforce from below. The trapped soldiers fight desperately against elementals already among them. These appear different from the ones Alice had encountered only yesterday. These were clearly meant for battle. They stand on four stocky legs allowing them to maintain balance even as they swing their oversize club like arms. Alice can see the careless strength of the stone creatures as men are sent flying from them with each horrible blow.

"We must aid them!" shouts Lowe.

"How? Their too close to the elementals! We'd just burn them too!" Alice replies, searching for some way to help.

There are only a few of the elementals against over a hundred soldiers but they seem more than enough. Standing much taller than even the largest Arsalian, they viciously attack anyone foolish enough to stray too near. Eventually, one knocks away the last soldier facing it and Alice immediately has Squiggles target the isolated elemental with a cry of "Infermious!"

The dragon dives in and roars at his foe, bathing it in fire as he passes. The elemental endures the fire stoically, even stopping as it burns, Squiggles' orange flames turning green as the magic animating the creature catches. Alice sees it quickly fall apart and begins searching for her next target. The soldiers, seeing this, make efforts to move away from the elementals, leaving them in the open and vulnerable. For all their strength, these elementals seem particularly slow but still manage to pin the soldiers against themselves and the inferno behind them. The moment an elemental is left in the open, Alice has Squiggles swoop down upon it, pouring a column of fire on its stone body.

She takes several down this way in as many minutes, but the losses to the infantry continue to mount. As she's lining Squiggles up for another dive, Lowe shouts, "LOOK OUT!"

Alice tries to turn her head but Lowe presses hard against her back, forcing her down. She sees the shadow of a large stone, easily as large as she is, sailing over her. It's so close she can feel the air being parted by it's passing, a horrible whistling accompanying it. A breath catches in Alice's throat as she watches the stone fly on and then down the mountain below. She looks to her right, where it must have come from, to see another heading her way. Squiggles doesn't seem to have noticed, more focused on his enemy, and Alice must get him to pull out of his dive to avoid the next stone.

She gets the dragon to climb and spots a small group of elementals, similar to the ones that ran away in the last battle. One of them hurls another stone but it doesn't have the distance. Knowing they'd been spotted, the hurlers begin to flee.

"They may be the leaders," suggests Lowe, "We should take them if we can, my lady."

Alice considers, looking back at the battle. Once the hurlers turned to flee, the four legged warrior elementals appear to have lost interest in the fight and even begin to crumble where they stand. The men begin to cheer their strange victory. With no further cause not to, Alice has Squiggles pursue the fleeing stone throwers.

These are smaller than the warriors and move with speed, but Squiggles is much faster. As he approaches, one of the elementals launches what looks like a forearm toward it's pursuer. Alice instinctually has Squiggles bank out of the way even though it is unlikely the stone missile would have hurt him. She loses ground doing so, but does it again when another stone is hurled. A third heads for them but this time Alice ignores it, gaining on them. A forth comes towards her and she intends to ignore this one too until she sees it arcing perfectly toward her head. Lowe's shield appears before her and the stone clangs loudly against it.

Alice gives him a quick nod of thanks and continues the pursuit, nearly upon the fleeing elementals, even as they head for the safety of thick trees. Alice is preparing to call for Squiggles' attack when the dragon suddenly bucks, roaring in surprise.

Squiggles cranes his neck back as Alice looks frantically around. Confused, Alice scans the sky, searching for what would have made the dragon react so. Feeling Squiggles about to maneuver, she tucks close to his body, screaming for Lowe to do the same. The knight hunkers down as they had practiced just as Squiggles whips around to face his attacker. Holding tight to the dragon's reigns, Alice can see the ground below has come alive with elementals, seemingly forming from the very earth. All begin hurling stones of various sizes at the dragon. Squiggles jolts several more times as he is hit while trying to find where his pain is coming from. Struck from all sides, the dragon becomes confused and ends up spiraling, losing altitude as he takes more hits. Too enraged by the attack, he no longer acknowledges Alice's direction even as she calls for him to climb to safety.

Squiggles wildly unleashes flame in his fury, batting away stones with his claws as he is steadily brought to the ground, his expansive wings taking numerous hits and struggling to keep him aloft. Alice screams for him to rise, beating her small fist on his great neck, but he doesn't listen. From the depths of her mind, horrible memories flash before her. Alice sees her mother, unresponsive on her bed as she wastes away before the pitiful cries of a much younger Alice. She hears Lowe shout something but is too distraught over the dragon's pain and her own haunted past to understand him.

Alice is suddenly shoved hard before his comforting, warm weight abruptly vanishes from her back. Alice looks to see she is alone atop the flailing dragon.

"Lowe?" Alice calls, then more urgently, "Lowe?!"

Her voice is drowned out by the raging roar of her dragon, biting and clawing at the stones assaulting him.

Alice screams, looking to the ground at the surrounding elementals, "LO-" a burst of agony resounds in her head and she recoils from it. A hand instinctively comes up to investigate under her helm and pulls away with blood. Her head reverberating with vicious pain, she looks around in the gathering darkness for some escape from it. Squiggles' own head jerks as a stone slams into his chin, cutting off his fierce battle cry, a spurt of flame blooming briefly from his nostrils. As the world slows and the darkness grows, they begin to fall.

Chapter 5
Rebellion

Alice sees her mother, lying still on her bed back home. It's hard to move but the young Tokala reaches and calls, "Mom. Mom!"

A rock lands in her path and she moves to avoid it but she's slow, strangely so. Alice looks at her feet, moving as if fighting a strong current. When she looks back to her mother, the bed has moved further away. Alice calls more urgently, trying to force her body to move faster. Then more rocks fall in her way. She has to look down to avoid them but every time she looks back to her mother, she's even further from reach. More rocks pile up before her and soon she's climbing over them, desperately trying to reach the bed. More and more rocks rain from the sky, forcing Alice to climb higher, blocking her mother from sight. Alice climbs frantically, rocks turning to larger stones as they fall all around her, walling her in. A darkness falls over her and she looks up to see a massive boulder tumbling right on top of her, she screams, "MOM!" just before it hits.

Alice awakens in darkness and pain. Her entire body aches horribly but more is the pounding in her head. She reaches for a spot just behind her right ear and recoils at the bloom of agony. The floor she lies on is cold and unforgivingly hard. She's struck with a jolt of fear when she blinks several times and sees only blackness. Terrified she's gone blind, Alice feels about her eyes to check if there's something over them. There isn't. Despite her throbbing body's demand that she lay still, Alice pushes off the stone floor with an elbow in an effort to get her arms and legs under her. The ache in her body triples and she only manages to roll over onto her belly before the pain forces her to stop. At least the cold floor felt nice against her aching head.

After a moment to collect herself, Alice rasps from a terribly dry throat, "Hello?"

Something moves.

Alice freezes when she hears a light shift in the air, then a swift pitter-patter like small feet. The sound quiets as if it's fleeing rather than approaching and Alice turns her head toward it, "Is, someone there? I, I need help."

Nothing.

Alice tries to moisten her mouth but her tongue feels like it's covered in thorns. As she tries to assess her condition, she suddenly remembers the battle. She rasps as loudly as she can, "Lowe? Squigs?"

Still nothing.

Cold, afraid, and hurt, Alice curls into herself in the absolute blackness trying to think, the only thing that didn't bring more pain. A strategy she had picked up when she was a child, she tries to recall a more pleasant place and a more pleasant time to take her from her current suffering. She finds memories of Danahlia and their time in the mountains, when they had no troubles and only each other to concern themselves with. Alice latches onto these memories, forcing herself to recall them in as much detail as possible, trying to replace her present, battered self with the one from years ago.

Alice isn't sure how long she's in the dark, but she has relived the joyous days she had spent with Danahlia several times over. She feels the warmth of those summer days they spent lazily sunbathing on a rock. She feels the security of her Liguna wrapped around her during the night. She even laughs recalling the lizard girl's antics and cries remembering their hardships. She sees her now, telling one of her wild stories while cooking something over a fire. Alice isn't really listening. She's too busy admiring Danahlia's smooth skin and the way her eyes sparkle in the firelight.

Danahlia looks to her, smiling, "Alice? Alice?" Alice feels herself being tugged away for the memory and tries even harder to focus on it. Danahlia's face becomes concerned and she calls more urgently, "Alice? Alice, can you hear me?" Alice wants to say she can, but her mouth doesn't work. Then to her horror, Danahlia begins to glow a bright green just before her skin bursts, consumed by emerald flames from within. She screams, "ALICE!"

Alice jolts awake to find the horrible green fire right before her eyes. She tries to move away but something holds her still. She whines pitifully, putting her hands over her face as someone says, "It's alright. Calm yourself." She continues to squirm and the voice assures, "Do not be afraid, you are not in danger here."

Alice tries to speak, but her throat is a crackly, prickly thing that stings with the effort. The voice calls for water. Something is put to Alice's lips and cool moisture drips into her mouth. Alice begins sucking greedily, letting the life saving liquid fill her mouth. It's taken from her when she begins to choke, coughing hoarsely and spitting it back up.

"Here," the voice says before murmuring, "Asendiote."

Alice feels her head and shoulders being lifted slightly as if set on a pillow of air. She's given water again and manages to drink. After a few gulps smooth the barbs in her throat, she looks to see a Murin sitting beside her, one with particularly large ears.

"Tw-twinkaleni?" Alice gasps.

The mage smiles, "Yes, it is I." She then leans over to examine the tender lump on Alice's head, "I was wondering when they'd send you against me."

Alice reaches for the Murin's face, unable to believe it's really her. The minor labor is exhausting and her hand falls limply to the hard ground she still lies on.

"Try not to move," says Twinkaleni, "You are still weak."

Alice is given more water and then sluggishly asks, "Wha, what happened? We, looked for you."

Twinkaleni nods, "I know. Rest now. All will be revealed in time."

Keeping her eyes open is becoming too taxing and Alice drifts off once more.

She awakens again in darkness but at least now she is on a layer of fur hides. Her head still pounds but the rest of her aches have dulled considerably. She is very hungry. Alice searches the darkness for Twinkaleni only to spot someone even smaller. A Lagomorph girl of perhaps five years. Her face is lit by some sparse, green light the rabbit child holds in her hands.

The Lagomorph is admiring the light when Alice weakly mumbles, "Hey."

The tiny girl looks up in surprise. Seeing Alice

looking at her, she immediately hops off the rock she had been sitting on and scampers away into blackness. Alice calls after her but she doesn't return. Alice finds her leather armor was removed though she is still clothed in what she wore the day of the battle. Finding the air over her fur blanket to be chilly, Alice wraps herself with the hides and slowly begins after the girl, tired of being in this dark place. A hand held out before her, she takes only a few slow steps before she hears someone coming.

Ahead, Alice sees a green light growing in strength, "Hello? Twinkaleni?"

The light stops before a young boy's voice calls back, "Nh, no."

As he gets closer, Alice sees he is a young Caprican, likely near ten. He holds out a few strips of dried meat. Alice's stomach burbles it's emptiness, the scent of food just reaching her, and the Tokala immediately approaches the boy.

"I'm suppose to give this to-" before the boy can finish, Alice snatches the meat and immediately begins tearing off pieces between her teeth. She barely tastes it, swallowing chunks whole in her desperation to get something into her. She begins to choke. The goat boy just looks at her, open mouthed, but the Lagomorph girl from before appears from behind him and offers a bowl of water. Alice drinks to dislodge the meat in her throat before eating more.

The Caprican starts to lead the rabbit girl away and Alice stops long enough to call to them with mouth full, "Don' go. Pleath."

They stop and turn back to her. Alice swallows hard and takes another drink, "I'm sorry, I'm just so hungry. I feel like I hadn't eaten in days."

"You haven't," says the boy.

"Yeah, I thought you were dead, but then you called for your mommy!" says the girl excitedly, skipping back to join her. In the faint green light, Alice can see they both wear tattered, drab robes similar to the ones the children from the Order of Thermathrogi wore. The Lagomorph girl stands beside her looking up with a wide grin, "You're pretty. I like your tail. It's very fluffy."

"Uh, thanks," says Alice, then looking to the

boy, asks, "Who are you? And where am I?"

The rabbit girl answers first, "I'm Tilly."

The boy points, saying, "She's Tilly. I'm Jacob. And we're in the-"

"The mountains!" Tilly announces.

"We're underground," adds Jacob.

"Where's Twinkaleni?" Alice asks as she eats.

"Fighting," says Jacob.

Alice looks to him, "Fighting? Fighting who?"

Jacob looks surprised, "Arsalia."

Alice gathers from the duo that they were being trained by the Order in two different cities when Twinkaleni began to appear. She told them of the terrible fate they would have if they stayed and that if they left with her they could be free from it. One night, Twinkaleni came with golems and smashed through the academy walls, taking the mages from the city. They hid under piles of rock during the day that Twinkaleni and other mages used to make their golems. At night, they would ride the golems until eventually reaching the relative safety of the mountains. There, Twinkaleni showed them new magic and the older mages learned to make their own golems.

"I can't make a golem yet," admits Tilly, "But Twinkaleni says if I practice, one day soon I will."

"What about the elementals?" asks Alice.

Tilly stumbles over the word while Jacob asks, "Elementals?"

Alice begins to piece things together, "The ones outside, the ones we've been fightin'... are, golems? How can...?" then she remembers her friends, "Where's Lowe? And Squiggles?" Her urgency surprises the children into silence and she tries again, more calmly, "Do you know what happened to the Lobovan that was with me, and my dragon?"

"That dragon was yours?" asks Tilly, eyes full of wonder.

The 'was' bothers Alice greatly and she asks, "Is he alive? Where is he?"

"We're not allowed to see it," says Jacob.

"Is he alive?" Alice presses.

Jacob shrugs, "I don't know. I only saw it when they brought it in. It looked hurt."

"I saw it too!" says Tilly, "It was soo big!"

"Can you take me to 'im?" Alice asks.

Jacob frowns, "We're not suppose to go near it."

"Yeah," Tilly agrees, "They said he might think we're food, and eat us."

"It's alright," comes Twinkaleni's voice as she steps into the chamber.

Alice quickly closes on the Murin, "Twinkaleni, what's goin' on? Where's Squiggles? And Lowe? Are they ok?"

"I am not aware of any Lowe but Squiggles is, intact," the Murin mage hesitates, "He was injured more than intended, but he does live."

Alice's eyes widen, "Intended? Were those your golems out there that attacked us?!"

Twinkaleni puts up placating hands, "A necessary evil I assure you. We only meant to make a show of knocking you down. I had hoped it would have been a simpler matter, but Squiggles has grown quite powerful since I saw him last. It had to be done."

"Why?!" barks Alice.

Twinkaleni's eyes narrow and her voice becomes stern, "I am fighting a war against a far greater enemy with very few resources. I cannot and do not wish to kill a nation's worth of people. Our only option is to break our enemy's spirit. I have now defeated Arsalia twice in the field and have taken their only dragon rider. We will only be free once their morale crumbles. Your fall has aided greatly in this."

This confuses Alice, "But what about the

elementals? Are they *all* golems? And the titan? They think one is attackin' Arsalia."

Twinkaleni allows herself a small smile, "As they are meant to."

Twinkaleni leads Alice through the dark with another glowing, green stone. Tilly and Jacob follow, listening to their savior's tale and likely hoping to see the illusive dragon being kept below the earth. Twinkaleni explains that since parting with Alice and Danahlia in Feoria, she had returned to the steam caves the girls had spent much of their time together near. She knew she had to uncover the great magic within the caves if she would ever be powerful enough to free her people, the magic wielders being kept enthralled by the Order of Thermathrogi.

She began by relentlessly excavating deeper and deeper into the mountains, steadily feeling the magic below getting stronger and stronger as she did. After a while, she encountered another elemental, which she managed to defeat with her golem, earning her another of the creatures' stone hearts. With practice and the magical energy within the caves being added to her own, she could eventually summon and maintain two golems at once. The deeper she delved into the depths of the Gadara Mountains, the more elementals she encountered. Defeating each earned her another stone heart, which the determined mage used to add more golems to her collection. With her knowledge and mastery of golems steadily increasing, she soon found it possible to control several of the stone constructs at the same time.

Twinkaleni stresses the effort it took to do it, but eventually she uncovered the rift she was certain was at the core of the mountains. Tilly asks and so Twinkaleni explains that a rift is believed to begin as a weak spot between their mortal world and the world of magic, Fayelindran. Continued pressure on this weak spot over many ages eventually breaks it, forming a hole between worlds. These holes are known as rifts, and it is thought that all the magic of this world originally came through them.

The rift Twinkaleni discovered pours an endless flood of magical energy into the bowels of the mountains. She says being around the rift is quite overwhelming and most are not allowed near it for their own safety. But those with the proper focus and respect can channel near limitless power from the rift, magnifying their own magical might many times over. With this discovery, Twinkaleni believed she now had the edge she needed to continue her mission of freeing the magically gifted from the chains of the Order.

Alice follows Twinkaleni down partially lit tunnels, the Murin explaining how she then began to liberate her fellow mages. She would approach an Order academy, much as Alice and she had done years before, to test the mages' receptivity to leaving. Once a few had agreed to do so, she would not make the mistake of sneaking back in to retrieve them as before. With powerful stone golems at her command, Twinkaleni would smash her way into a city, and then target locations not likely to be heavily populated in the middle of the night. She spread the damage as far as she could so that the Arsalians would not uncover her true intent when she also struck the academies. She would break down the Order's high walls to take as many mages as would come before fleeing the city, leaving only destruction and confusion in her wake.

Each academy struck added mages to her cause. She would teach them the power to craft their own golems, and with them, continue to liberate her kind. But a significant problem was that the renegade mages' strength relied greatly on the mountains. Here, they could hide among the caves, train with the rift's power, and survive off the bounty of the mountains' vast forests. This dependence would make it very difficult for them to liberate the mages in cities further south, which was most of Arsalia. Twinkaleni had already struck those they could and has begun reaching further out, but doing so posed tremendous risk and they simply did not have the numbers to allow it.

Twinkaleni is aware her rebellion is outnumbered by Arsalian soldiers many hundreds to one if even only northern and central Arsalia are rallied against them. Alice knows from her briefs with Lord Alvaro that western Arsalia is on watch for any aggressive moves by Feoria while they wish to keep the south in reserve to back the west if it becomes necessary. Twinkaleni has already surmised that this would be the case and also feels that if she attacked too boldly, Arsalia would focus less on Feoria and more on her. She was staging a careful balancing act of luring Arsalia's armies to her while not posing so great a threat that the entire nation rises up and washes over her tiny rebellion.

She could not face Arsalia's might directly but she could chip away at it over time. Her only hope of success was to keep her much larger enemy off balance with uncertainty and surprise.

Alice asks about the titan Alvaro is certain he saw. Twinkaleni says that her time around the rift has given her access to tremendous power and she had been the one to raise the titan. Fueled by the rift's limitless energy and her own will, she turned the entire peak of a mountain into a gigantic golem and crushed the first army she lured with it. That was the first and last time she had used such power, as it was an excruciatingly taxing process. But it had served it's purpose of alarming Arsalia while forcing them to call upon the only dragon rider left to them. Dragons were the only things known to have ever defeated a titan after all.

"And now they have seen their champion fall, and not even to a titan," says Twinkaleni, taking them down another roughly hewn corridor, "Their spirits lowered, the entire army has elected to retreat to the base of the mountains."

"Then, you killed all those men, with your boulders and golems?" Alice asks in disbelief, recalling the crushed and the anguished cries of those wounded in the attacks.

Twinkaleni turns on her, "They are soldiers, Alice! The moment their superiors realize who they truly face, do you think any of them will hesitate to cut me down, or Tilly, or Jacob?! We are property to them. Disobedient slaves at best.

"But is it worth it?" Alice shoots back, "To kill so many people?"

"Are you asking if living free to make your own decisions and not having your life used up by someone else is worth fighting for? You saw but a fleeting glimpse of what it is like for us in the Order. I do not expect you to understand what we have all managed to live through," says Twinkaleni, gesturing to the younger mages, "But know that each and every mage that has joined me did so by choice. I have told them of the dangers we face and the struggle we will have to endure, and they still chose to come. Not one of them is forced to fight for me as they would have been under an Arsalian flag."

"But the men you kill. They're fathers, brothers, and sons," Alice protests.

"They are soldiers. They made the choice to be soldiers. They could fight for their own freedom if they chose, but they choose to fight for Arsalia. And at this moment in time, Arsalia is my enemy," states Twinkaleni, turning back to lead them through a cavern.

"Not everyone has a choice," counters Alice, thinking of the conscription notice that was prepared for her father should she refuse to fight for Arsalia herself, "They would have had my dad in the army if I didn't come here to fight your titan. They said they'd execute me for treason because I helped you before."

Twinkaleni doesn't turn back to her, "Then your choice was to fight them or to fight a titan. I would think facing an army of men from atop a dragon would be the easier battle. But all the same, I am glad you came."

"So you could make a big show of hurting Squigs and me?" Alice spits hotly.

"No," Twinkaleni replies upon entering a great chamber, "Because we *need* you."

In dim green light Alice can just make out Squiggles on the far side lying still. She runs to him calling the dragon's name. He turns his massive head to the sound and makes a happy rumble in his throat. He rises slowly and Alice can see he is in pain. He limps with one foreclaw held close to his chest and a wing bent awkwardly, unable to close all the way. Alice runs faster, ignoring her own pain so the dragon doesn't have to move any further. She puts both arms around his snout and hugs his nose, the dragon cool and firm.

"I thought I lost you, Boy," Alice cries.

He sniffs her and then blows hot, moist air from his nostrils, rumbling his joy.

"Why's he in here? Why isn't anyone helpin' 'im?" Alice demands of Twinkaleni.

"None have the skill to treat him I'm afraid," Twinkaleni admits, approaching the dragon with the two younger mages, "Though he is healing rather quickly. He was much worse when we retrieved him. As to why he is here," Twinkaleni says placing a hand on the great reptile's muzzle, "Obviously so he could recover, and be here when you did."

"There was a Lobovan riding with us. Did you bring him too?" Alice asks, not letting go of her dragon.

"Our efforts were entirely focused on retrieving the two of you. I don't recall another," Twinkaleni replies.

Alice's heart drops. A flash of memory reminds her of Lowe, shoving her forward before he disappeared. She hadn't seen it but is somehow certain the fool had been trying to protect her and is likely dead because if it, buried under falling stones.

"So you killed him too," mutters Alice.

Twinkaleni sighs, "The losses of any war are regrettable. I would see this conflict ended as soon as possible."

"But *you* started it!" shouts Alice, startling the younger mages, though Twinkaleni seemed to be expecting it.

"Not true," she says sternly, petting the

dragon, "This war started the moment Arsalia's ungifted elite began to enslave our power for their own will. To use *us* to take what *they* wanted. To warp *us* to fit *their* desires. To *kill us* when they felt we were unwilling to *sacrifice* ourselves for *them*. It has only taken centuries of torment for us to have this one chance to make a stand. We will *not* be their slaves, their tools, their weapons any longer."

"What are you gonna do then?" Alice asks hotly, "Kill everyone in Arsalia until they say sorry?"

Twinkaleni keeps her voice even, "No. My goal was never violence. I only wish to offer a chance of freedom to those who would seek it. I want to speak to all the oppressed mages of Arsalia and see if they will not join me in creating a better life for themselves. A life free of the propaganda fed to them by the Order. A life where their future is not already decided. A life where they can seek happiness and fulfillment without it being hammered into their minds what those should be. A life where they are able to say 'no.' A life of choice."

"Sounds like a lot," says Alice, cradling Squiggles' head, "How're you gonna give 'em all that?"

"For now, the task is to break the Arsalian army's spirit, force them to retreat back to the safety of their cities. From there, I was hoping I could count on you for support in-"

"Why would I help you?" Alice demands, "I'm not a mage. Those are *my* people you're killing out there."

"Who is the they that threatened your father with conscription? That threatened you with execution?" asks Twinkaleni.

"I don't know, someone named Lady Huld. She signed the letter," says Alice.

"A Lady. A noble," spits Twinkaleni, "An elite in Arsalian society. Did she offer you something for your services, or was being allowed to keep your head reward enough?"

Alice narrows her eyes at the Murin, remembering the letter, "She said if I beat the titan, she'd give me land and make me a lady, too."

"A vassalage," Twinkaleni states, "Which

means you would be in service to this Lady Huld. She intends to use you, Alice, for her own gain. Even if you defeated the titan and returned to her a great hero, she would only use you again and again to fight her enemies."

"What enemies? We're only fightin' you," claims Alice.

"You cannot be so naive," retorts Twinkaleni, "Recall what Danny once said about soldiers killing her family during the onset of the Blood War?" Alice did remember that and Twinkaleni continues, "I am convinced the entire conflict was orchestrated by Arsalia, perhaps even partly by your Lady Huld."

That seems absurd to Alice, "Why would anyone have *wanted* to start the Blood War?"

"Consider King Ghadhanfar's death," urges Twinkaleni, "It was a strange occurrence for one still in his prime, young enough even to leave no heir. With the line of succession broken, the seat of power over all of Arsalia was left to anyone with the strength to claim it. Such a thing has and would have again led to a civil war that would have torn Arsalia to shreds, leaving it vulnerable to Feoria. I believe the Royal Council, that took governance over Arsalia in the absence of a king, began the Blood War in order to buy themselves time to weaken their opposition." Alice looks at the Murin confused, as she continues, "By spreading rumor that Cold Bloods had slain their king, all the territories would unite against a singular enemy. Anyone who did not would have been considered a traitor. An extended conflict with Feoria would weaken both nations, but those of the Royal Council would naturally have the edge, already seated high above most others. They would simply watch as the other great houses spent their strength in the war, while those on the council would consolidate their own. Once the war was over, their former rivals would be too weak to oppose them and Feoria would be temporarily nullified. I believe it is only a matter of time before the members of the Royal Council turn upon each other."

Remembering what Lowe had said, Alice murmurs, "Lady Huld is part of that Royal Council."

Twinkaleni nods, "Then it is likely as I thought. She has found the opportunity she waited for to acquire you. With you and your dragon at her command, she would have the advantage over her co-conspirators. Once my rebellion is quelled, a new war would rise in the heart of Arsalia. Huld would use you to defeat her enemies and place herself on the throne as queen."

Alice's immediate thought is, "That's crazy. Why would anyone start wars, kill so many people, just so they can sit on some fancy chair?"

Twinkaleni begins to rub one of her exceptionally large ears between two fingers, "There is no greater lure in this world than that of power. You must understand, to an ambitious noble, to society's elite, the lives of other people are nothing. They live in this world with the firm belief that their very birth makes them superior to any other. They are raised to measure the worth of others by how much they stand to gain from their rival's expenditure."

Twinkaleni made these people sound like monsters. Alice has trouble believing it and asks, "How would you know all that?"

"By living it," Twinkaleni says simply, "Every mage freed from the Order knows of this. Even you have seen it, the contempt and total disregard for any life they cannot control."

Alice is reminded of the man in the pixie forest, the deserter. A bad man perhaps, but one who hid in fear for his life knowing if he was found, he would be executed for leaving the army. Then of Lyca and the forest children, the way the agent of the Order had so carelessly killed them and justified it by calling them draft dodgers. And the way the Order took childrens' lives away to turn them into weapons to fight in their wars. Her own father was sent away to fight in a war that, if Twinkaleni was right, people like Lady Huld started. Could it all be true? Could these 'elite' people really care so little about others that they could torture children and start wars, destroy families and even countries to get what they wanted? Alice finds it difficult to believe that any person would be so vile, but here she was, sent under threat of death and the death of her father to fight in a war she had nothing to do with. Could it all be because of people like Huld?

Such people must be very powerful to be able to do so much and Alice wonders, "You said you wanted me to help, but what can I do about it? I'm no mage. I'm just, me."

Twinkaleni looks at Alice in surprise, "You are the only dragon rider in all of Arsalia. The kingdoms that compose Arsalia were originally claimed ages ago by people just like you. A dragon is worth more than any army in the field. Should you choose it, you could reforge Arsalia to your will."

"No, no." Alice shakes her head, imagining where such a path might lead, "I don't want to kill people."

Twinkaleni looks to Alice earnestly, "Then join me in liberating mine. Once we are free to do so, we will leave these lands for good. We will build a new society in the Wildlands, perhaps even beyond, where Arsalia cannot touch us. One free of oppression and greed. One were leadership and standing are earned through contribution, not granted by birthright." Twinkaleni gestures to the two younger mages, having hesitantly made their way to Squiggles and now tentatively reach out for him, "These things do not come without cost. Our struggle will be long and difficult. Having you and Squiggles as allies would ease it considerably."

Alice rests her head on the dragon, watching the children pet him, undisguised awe on their faces, "I don't know. I want to help free the mages, but Arsalia is my home. Wouldn't that make me a traitor?"

"Have you ever pledged your allegiance to Arsalia? To one of it's Lords perhaps?" Twinkaleni asks. Alice hadn't so the Murin wonders, "Then what oath could you break? What words could you be accused of going back on?" Alice can't answer and the mage continues, "Do you feel obligated to give your life and service to some noble you've never met simply because you were born in a land they *claim* to own? Perhaps they've earned your loyalty when they so generously aided you after you lost your mother and were left alone in the world."

"No noble ever helped me," spits Alice, feeling the struggle of her youth being diminished by the thought.

"No, they didn't," says Twinkaleni, looking over the massive dragon before her, "So how could you be a traitor to a country that never earned your loyalty? That, in fact, threatens your very life and that of your family."

Alice isn't sure, but then considers, "What

about my dad? They threatened to make him fight again. And Danny, if they find out she has a connection to us, they might go after her too."

"Danny will be fine in Feoria, and your father would be most welcome among us," Twinkaleni assures.

"She isn't *in* Feoria," Alice corrects.

Twinkaleni's large, round ears perk up as Alice explains what has been going on with the Liguna since they parted company. The Murin mage takes this in, rubbing her ears once more, "I see. And you feel Danny will not be persuaded to leave Arsalia?"

"I don't think so. She wants to preserve the peace between the nations," says Alice, checking on Squiggles' wounds. His scales are cracked and shattered in some spots, but the flesh beneath is mending. This makes Alice wonder, "How long has it been since you brought me here?"

Without looking up from her pondering, Twinkaleni says, "Thirteen days."

"Thirteen?!" Alice blurts, unable to believe she

had been out so long, "How can... what's been goin' on out there? Have more people died?"

Twinkaleni looks angrily at Alice, but then takes a calming breath before saying, "We have beaten them back for now. The army regroups at the foot of the mountains. This has bought us a moment's breath."

Alice feels around one of Squiggles wounds and the dragon rumbles in protest, "What happens now?"

"*We* must prepare our defenses for the next bout," says Twinkaleni, "You are no prisoner. You are free to go when you wish. I would very much like to have your support, Alice, but I understand that it is much to ask. Squiggles needs time to heal, perhaps you could use this to consider your options."

Alice looks at the mage children, marveling at the dragon, "What if I wanna help?"

Twinkaleni is turned away from her but Alice is certain she hears a smile when the Murin says, "Then we must devote time to figuring out how best you can."

Chapter 6
The Future

Even without the commitment from Alice to join her, Twinkaleni is excited by the prospect and immediately begins coming up with ideas of how to make the most of such an alliance. Since Arsalia is yet unaware of the mages' roll in the current conflict, Twinkaleni believes this ignorance can be further played to her advantage with Alice's help. The mage had first made her attacks on cities look almost savage, with only a hint of tact. Then, she lured the first army sent against her into a very basic trap, and the second into a number of them, each time showing Arsalia that their enemy was more clever than they previously thought. This would keep them less sure of themselves and hesitant to act more aggressively.

As Twinkaleni is explaining this, another mage, this one an Echanian girl, rushes into the chamber under the light of another glowing, green stone. Breathing hard, she informs Twinkaleni that someone named Sven is back.

Twinkaleni's eyes widen, ears perking up as she asks, "Was he successful?"

Trying to catch her breath, the horse girl can only nod. Twinkaleni immediately begins toward the way the Echanian came in. Alice and the others leave Squiggles to rest so they can follow. The heaving girl tells Twinkaleni that eight more have joined them. When Alice asks what's going on, Twinkaleni explains that she had sent a couple of the more skilled mages following her to Norwood to contact those held there in another of the Order's academies. They began the operation even as the second coalition force was being amassed under Lord Alvaro. Working right under the army's nose, Sven's team had apparently convinced eight more mages to join her cause.

Twinkaleni hurries through a tunnel, Alice and the other mages following, until they reach the mouth of the cave. A handful of people, varying in species and mostly younger than Alice, have gathered to greet their returned comrades as well as the new members they have brought. Sven turns out to be another Murin of plain gray fur who appears to be a bit older than Twinkaleni. The moment she finds him, Twinkaleni runs over to Sven, embracing him warmly. This makes Alice smile. As long as she had known the small mouse mage, Twinkaleni had always shied away from physical contact. The other mage must mean a great deal for her to forgo her usual avoidance.

After some words are exchanged between them, Sven addresses the other mages in a surprisingly deep voice, "Free mages *formerly* of Arsalia, this is Twinkaleni Orbear. It is she who broke free from the Order to discover the truth of our bondage. It is she who now seeks to free us all. Will you join her in liberating the rest of our brothers and sisters?"

The new mages give there ascent and Twinkaleni steps forth, "We have come a long way in a very short time. In only months, many of us have thrown down the chains that have been forced upon our kind for hundreds of years. In this act, we show Arsalia who we are. Are we slaves?"

Sven and the other mages shout, "No!"

Twinkaleni asks, "Have we masters?"

The new rebels join in, "No!"

"Are we free?!"

All the mages cheer, "Yes!"

Twinkaleni shouts over them, "NO! We are not!" the others quite and the mage leader tells them, "As long as Arsalia has an army raised against us, we *will* be hunted. We will be forced to fight or hide. We will not be free." Concerned looks are shared by the mages as she continues, "But we, only numbering in the dozens, have already defeated Arsalia's armies!"

Sven enthusiastically adds, "And yet again!" As attention falls to him he announces, "In rescuing our newest brothers and sisters, we set fire to Arsalia's supply base in Norwood! On our return, we saw Arsalia's army, thousands strong, fleeing in panic from the foot of the mountains!"

The mages cheer, disbelief and joy in their voices while Twinkaleni has more words with Sven. Alice watches as the Murin pair share news, unheard over the others, but it seems to be very good from Twinkaleni's smile. Alice is amazed at how Twinkaleni has grown. She isn't the vertically challenged, little girl Alice had once traveled with years ago. She is a woman now, leading a rebellion against an entire nation. And from the looks of it, she's succeeding.

The mage leader quiets the others down with a raise of her tiny hands, "Once more Arsalia flees before us!" She allows the mages to cheer some before saying, "But our struggle is far from over! They will return. And we *will* be ready for them. Each defeat weakens their resolve," Twinkaleni walks over to the newest additions to her rebellion, "And each academy struck frees more of our people," she then looks over all those gathered, "But we still have much to do, for I did not begin this fight to free only the north. I will continue my campaign against Arsalia's tyranny until all mages are free!"

The mages cheer once more and a simple celebration begins as the newest mages introduce themselves to the others and all rejoice over the news that Arsalia's army is on the run. Alice has to tell several of them that she isn't a mage when they greet her with a physical gesture but don't feel her aura, or when they wonder which academy she was freed from. This makes them look at her strangely but Twinkaleni soon returns with Sven. She introduces her to him as a dear old friend and

Arsalia's only dragon rider. He immediately wonders if the mages will be counting her as an ally, though Twinkaleni says Alice is still undecided.

"With Sven's success, it appears Arsalia is pulling back from the mountains, likely to fortify their cities against further attack. This will give us more time to plan, and you, more time to consider your path," informs Twinkaleni.

Sven looks to Alice, "Yours would be a tremendous aid to us. Please consider it."

Alice frowns, still afraid to commit to anything. She fears for her father, for Danahlia, for Squiggles, for Ashleigh, for Twinkaleni, for the mages, and all those who could be terribly affected by what she chooses to do. And she hates to admit it, with so many around her willing to sacrifice so much, but she also fears for herself. What will happen if she chooses to fight for Arsalia, her home? She will likely have to kill the mages she stood among now, maybe even Twinkaleni. If she decided to fight with them for their freedom, she would be betraying her own people, branded a traitor, and never allowed to set foot in Arsalia again. Her father may be killed, Danahlia too, and of course, she might as well. What if she fought for no one? Simply took her father and left Arsalia for good. With Squiggles, they could survive anywhere. Would they be hunted? What would happen to her friends? Would Danahlia be ok? Could Twinkaleni succeed without her? These are some of the questions Alice struggles with for several days while staying with the mages.

Now up and about, Twinkaleni is eager to show Alice what she had accomplished in the time since she'd returned to Arsalia. Many of the stones in this area of the mountains were painstakingly extracted from deep within the earth, where they had been exposed to the mysterious rift's energy for ages. They had never formed into elementals but still housed great pools of magical energy that the mages could tap into to fuel their own power. Originally pulled up to make training easier for those learning to create golems, Twinkaleni, now beyond the need for even stone hearts to form her own, found she could use the magic infused stones to channel the rift's energy, even from a fair distance. This allowed her to create her army crushing titan.

She admits hers may not have been as impressive as the titan she had seen while in Alice's company years back, but it did serve admirably in it's purpose. A problem, however, was that even the stones would only allow her to direct the rift's energy from so far. This meant her titan would only be available to the mages' efforts as long as they stayed in very close proximity to the rift that powers it. Twinkaleni explains that now that they have hit Norwood, they have put Arsalia on the defensive, but have also reached a limit to how far south they can safely strike.

The Order of Thermathrogi has academies in many large cities all over Arsalia, each containing mages that will potentially join Twinkaleni's fight for freedom. She wishes to aid them all but the mages only have the advantage when close to the Gadara Mountains. Traveling further south meant being away from safety for longer, increasing the chances of being discovered. If a freed mage were captured, their torture would clear the cloud of illusion the rebels have worked so hard to maintain. As it is, Arsalia thinks it faces stone monsters, slowly revealing a disturbing level of intelligence. This keeps them wary and hesitant to act. But if they ever found out it was all magic and trickery, the rebellion would be crushed under Arsalia's fury. This is what Twinkaleni most desires Alice's aid in. Squiggles would give the mages secure and swift access to all of the academies across Arsalia.

"So you don't want me to fight?" Alice asks while Twinkaleni shows her how the mages process the mountains' game for storage in the naturally cool caves all over the range.

"I will not deny that battle may be an inevitable component," admits Twinkaleni, handing Alice a load of dried meat to bring to Squiggles, "But consider that you would be fighting no matter which side you choose. Siding with Arsalia would mean you would face me. If you told Arsalia's command all you knew of us, their army would crush us easily. Would you want to be responsible for the deaths of so many who only seek to be free?"

"No. But if what I know is so important, why are you showing me all this?" wonders Alice.

Twinkaleni smiles, "Because in the years we have spent traveling together, I feel I've gotten to know the kind of individual you are."

"Really?" smirks Alice.

Twinkaleni nods as they head to Squiggles'

chamber, "Indeed. And I believe you will side with us as you have already done in the past. All that keeps you from doing so now is the concern you have for those you care for. You are a good person, Alice. You would risk yourself to protect those you love and even those you feel have been wronged. Unfortunately, in this conflict, I like to think both sides have people you care for. Both causes you would fight for."

"I don't know what to do," admits Alice.

"Then may I offer a suggestion?" asks Twinkaleni. Alice looks to the rebellious Murin as she says, "Squiggles heals quickly, perhaps an effect of the magic infused stones he prefers to consume. He will be ready to take flight soon. Take him to your father and Danny. Perhaps you could convince them to stay in Feoria for a time. Under Danny's uncle's protection, they would be safe. You could stay with them if you truly do not wish to be a part of this conflict."

Having her father and Danahlia remain in Feoria did seem like a good plan. Alice had already come to the conclusion that she could not just sit idly by while her friend fought a battle against insurmountable odds, and so Alice agrees to make the attempt once Squiggles has healed.

The dragon rests in his cavern, getting stronger by the day. Alice thinks Twinkaleni may be right about the magic stones helping him recover. He definitely prefers them over others. These and the other glowing stones all the mages seem to posses are pieces from those brought from deep underground. Charged over the ages by the rift's energy, they contain a great deal of raw earth magic, making them excellent tools for teaching the growing rebellion how to create golems. All the talk of the mysterious rift has Alice very curious about it and she is eventually led to see it.

Twinkaleni has made her own tunnels down to the rift. The natural ones leading to it being long, winding, and "inefficient." Hers, meticulously plotted while intersecting and utilizing some of the natural ones, are far more direct but still take some time to travel through. The tunnel Twinkaleni leads Alice down cuts through a few chambers the mages are using for practice. With Arsalia beaten back for now, they must make the most of their time, each working hard to master the skills they need to face the armies sent against them. Even the youngest mages are given Earth stones, those infused with magic, to help them become accustomed to channeling the energies that will allow them to make their golems. Little Tilly happily demonstrates she can make her stone glow bright green with focus.

More adept mages are given heart stones, taken from the elementals found deeper underground. With these and the guidance of the more experienced, like Sven, they can make their first attempts at summoning forth their own golems. Similar to Pebbles, Twinkaleni's first golem, they are small and shaky, but the closer to the rift Alice and Twinkaleni venture, the larger and louder they become. Advanced mages can be seen and most definitely heard in other chambers where they spar with their golems in mock battles, testing design and skill. The golems constructed by the mages do not have a uniform shape or size but rather reflect their creators' ideas of what will be most effective in battle. Some have long swinging arms for flailing at their opponents, while others are more compact and seem made for ramming like living siege engines.

The closer to the rift the mages are, the more

rift energy they are able to channel, increasing their powers and greatly reducing the time it takes to master their abilities. Some, like Twinkaleni, are even able to maintain several golems at once. The echoing crash of impact from battles involving multiple golems is incredible, but nothing compared to the demonstration in which Twinkaleni battles Sven.

Sven is older and bigger than Twinkaleni, but the younger Murin has far more experience with golems. In their bout, the two stand on opposite sides of a large cavern. Those not occupied with setting up defenses across the mountains, mostly the younger mages, are gathered to watch. Twinkaleni begins by summoning a single modest golem without using a heart stone, while Sven tosses out several, summoning four bulky golems to challenge it. The four spread out to surround their single enemy. Twinkaleni's waits patiently. Sven's golems hesitate for a moment before, in an impressive display of agility, one leaps into the air over Twinkaleni's while the other three charge in directly. With speed and strength, the smaller golem steps under the one leaping at it, grabs it's stubby feet, and slams the larger creature into one of it's counter parts with such force that the leaper shatters with a deafening smash.

Among the observes are a few more advanced mages who protect the others huddled to watch. They use their magic to catch or redirect stray stones from them while the others look on in awe as Twinkaleni's golem is assaulted by the other three. Twinkaleni's golem is smaller but she manipulates it with speed and precision, letting it slip past the great hammering fists of its rivals. Pound after earth shattering pound is dodged by the nimbler golem. Sven tosses out two more stone hearts. The glowing, green stones immediately become encased in the abundant rock of the cavern, becoming two more golems. Alice notices Sven's eyes have also changed. Typically black, they now seemed to be clouded in shadow that reaches out to the very air. Even the golem Twinkaleni first destroyed begins to reconsolidate itself anew. Outnumbering their prey, Sven's six golems converge on Twinkaleni's.

The mage leader does not let herself become surrounded again. Instead, her golem charges and leaps into one of Sven's. They smash together with a resounding thud, before stone and rock crackle and shift. Twinkaleni's golem and Sven's seem to meld into one larger golem. This one turns on the others and they begin smashing at each other with stone powdering force. Alice and the others cover their ears as they watch the clash of the stone goliaths. Twinkaleni's eyes change as well, now glowing their eerie golden color. As her golem smashes through Sven's, it becomes larger, adding parts of it's fallen foes to itself. Sven's do the same, repurposing his own fallen golems. At the climax of the bout, two massive behemoths are left to wrestle for dominance. Limbs change shape as stone crumbles, sledgehammers becoming wedges that seek to sever arms and legs, as others grow long to reach and entangle.

Both golems take a tremendous amount of punishment but continue to reform. Looking at the too competing mages, the battle seems to be more one of focus and endurance, seeing who can simply outlast the other. They make gestures in the air with their hands, Sven almost mimicking his golem, while Twinkaleni's are more subdued. Sven's golem gets Twinkaleni's in a sort of bear hug and manages to squeeze it in half. But Twinkaleni's golem's leg like appendages, wrap around Sven's while the torso uses many arms to climb over and simply envelope the top of the other. After some obvious strain, Sven concedes, falling to his knees. Twinkaleni, apparently now in control of the last melded monstrosity of a golem, takes a slight bow, her golem making a deeper one to the audience of young cheering mages. Alice doesn't cheer. The glow in the mages' eyes worries her too much.

Twinkaleni lets the last golem crumble as she approaches the younger mages, excitedly talking among themselves, "You see what can be accomplished with only a few months of dedication? Sven proves that a free mage, devoted to his cause, is easily worth more than a hundred of Arsalia's finest soldiers."

"As you, are worth a thousand," pants Sven, coming to join her.

Twinkaleni smiles, "Together, we have beaten back two armies already. And with each mage we liberate, we grow stronger as Arsalia grows weaker. The more powerful we become the sooner we will be free of them. The sooner our lives will be our own."

"So we must work hard, knowing the fate of all our kind rests with us!" Sven finishes.

The young mages give a little cheer and begin to disperse, even more eager to learn to wield the awesome power of their leaders. Sven and the other advanced mages take the younger ones to continue their training while Twinkaleni rejoins Alice. Concerned over the glow in the dueling mages' eyes, Alice asks about a subject that had been largely avoided ever since it was first witnessed. Twinkaleni says they were taught by the Order to believe the glow was caused by demons that lived within them, the supposed source of their power. They were told that when it happened it meant the demon was gaining strength as the mage lost focus and control. If not kept contained, the demon could possess fully the mage's body and do unspeakable things. The Order would have no choice but to execute such a mage. As such, those that allowed the glow to occur were severely punished.

The talk of demons worries Alice even more, particularly after witnessing the things Twinkaleni was capable of when the glow occurred. Twinkaleni, however, just laughs at the idea and that she ever believed in such nonsense. As with much of what the Order had taught them, it was a lie. After experiencing the phenomenon many times, the Murin mage is certain the emission is from an abundance of mana, magical energy, being channeled by a mage. Concentrated mana tends to glow, and brighter the more there is. She relates this to the subtle glow of the core stones found in jellies, the fiery orange light of the emberstones the girls had encountered in the Great Horn Mountain, and the green emanation of the stone hearts found in the elementals. Twinkaleni imagines if they were translucent like jellies, a mage's entire body might glow during moments of intense spell casting. This soothes Alice considerably, after all she had seen many magical things glow, like the pixies of the jelly forest, the light sprites of the Great Horn, and even her own sword.

Now that it was out in the open, Alice asks about it on their way to the rift. She tells Twinkaleni how worried Danahlia and she used to get when they saw it. Twinkaleni says she was unaware of the glow occurring for the most part and says to Alice's question that her vision does not change in any way when it does. Alice describes the times the Murin's eyes glowed their fierce golden color and Twinkaleni concludes that it seems likely that it occurred then because of her reckless gathering of too much energy, likely a result of her anger. Because of this, they decide to call the phenomenon, *mana fury*.

Getting deeper into the mountains, Alice notices Twinkaleni's breathing becoming heavier. Not labored but more like she smells something wonderful and wishes to fill her lungs with whatever aroma is so inciting. Alice only smells damp, musty earth. Twinkaleni grins, saying they are getting closer. They travel alone here, the younger mages forbidden from coming this far, and the older ones busy with other tasks. According to Twinkaleni, the rift produces an infinite flow of raw mana that could easily overwhelm an unprepared mage. Alice remembers that Twinkaleni uses her magic to reach out and gather energy from the environment, taking in wind for air magic, heat for fire, and needing a source of water to manipulate that element. It has to come from somewhere for her to use it. Twinkaleni says that there is so much mana flowing in from the rift that if a mage were not careful, they might literally explode.

Twinkaleni seems to truly enjoy it here, practically bouncing with each step while taking in deep breaths as one might upon entering a bakery. Alice asks how it feels and Twinkaleni describes it by saying each breath is like filling your lungs after being under water for several minutes, like filling your stomach after days of hunger, like waking up after a good night's rest, all while relaxing in a hot spring. Alice feels nothing but cool clammy air and is a little jealous of the mouse mage's comfort. Twinkaleni's eyes even begin to glow their bright golden color despite her apparent elation. She says the mana from the rift is trying to fill her as it does the rock around them, giving them power. Alice had thought the steadily stronger green glow was from Twinkaleni's magic but eventually notices it is coming from the very walls of the tunnel. It doesn't become overly bright by any means but one would not need a torch here to find their way.

Twinkaleni says she must be careful not to allow too much of the rift's energy to fill her, as it would be like trying to swallow all the water of a river, but admits the curious sensation of wanting to anyway. Alice wonders if it is safe to go on further. Twinkaleni assures it is and that they wouldn't actually be getting all that close to the rift itself, as it remained heavily guarded by elementals. Remembering her last encounter with one of the earth born monsters, this makes Alice rather nervous. Squiggles is still resting closer to the surface. The Murin mage confidently says it will be fine and that she had been down this way many times already.

Alice begins to feel a strange tingling buzz that grows as does the strength of the green glow emanating from the surrounding rock. It feels somewhat like when her foot falls asleep, only all over. Wondering about this, Twinkaleni says she doesn't feel it, but has been wondering what would happen if one without the touch of magic was ever this close to the rift. The sensation, subtle at first, is getting uncomfortable and Alice wonders if she should continue when their tunnel gives way to a gargantuan chamber.

They enter onto a small plateau. All around them the rock is aglow with green light like a fog that hugs the floor, walls, and ceiling. Immediately, Alice spots what must be the rift, the source of all the wondrous magic in this place. She had never seen anything like it and her mind struggles to comprehend what she is witness to. At first it appears as an extremely elaborate spider's web, though spherical rather than planar. Wisps of white light emerge from all over, reaching out to the massive chamber it inhabits. It's as if these bright threads suspend it high in the open air, but each thread moves. Some have anchored in spots, wobbling to and fro like steam, while others drift lazily about the chamber, perhaps in search of their own anchor. The whole of it seems to spiral and shift in a slow dance though it remains hovering in place.

The light of the rift's center is as pure white as a star, illuminating the center of the chamber with it's brilliant glow. It mixes with the green flowing out of the earth around it. Alice notices the green light shifts as it mingles with the white but not in sync with it. She looks closer at this for a while before realizing why. The floor of this massive chamber, stretching far off into a green glowing haze, is covered with elementals. Alice's breath catches, a shiver running through her, and she immediately backs into the tunnel, trying to pull Twinkaleni with her. But the Murin assures that they are safe.

"They seem drawn to the power that created them," says Twinkaleni dreamily, her eyes glowing bright, "Isn't it beautiful?"

"Uh, yeah," says Alice, a bit more concerned about the elementals.

It is difficult to see individuals, their dark,

blocky silhouettes so tightly packed against the green and white light of the chamber, but there may be hundreds of them. They shift a little, occasionally bumping into each other but mostly seem to stand still as if in awe of the rift's power. The largest of them, standing several stories, are closest to the rift but still can't manage to reach it. They don't even seem to try, content just be in its presence. Twinakleni says that when provoked, they attack as fiercely as the first the girls had ever seen but for the most part stay peaceful. She has taken more than a few stone hearts from these creatures but hasn't put even a dent in their numbers. Alice worries over them emerging from this chamber and attacking the mages, though Twinkaleni assures her tunnels are small enough that they cannot use them. The natural tunnels could lead them to the surface but their winding length has yet to do so.

The tingly feeling Alice has been experiencing becomes even more unpleasant. The pair gather as many of the glowing green stones as they can, Twinkaleni using magic to float a great many, and head back up. The stones will act as portable pockets of energy for the training mages to draw from as well as provide a snack for Squiggles.

As the dragon continues to recover over the next few days, Twinkaleni comes up with a way for Alice to contribute to the war effort while not engaging in direct combat with Arsalia. When Alice is preparing to depart with Squiggles,Twinkaleni reveals that she plans to act as an emissary for the elementals and titan Arsalia believes it is fighting.

"You want to talk to them?" asks Alice, dumbfounded, "But the Order knows who you are. Won't they just take you back or kill you?"

Twinkaleni smirks, "I doubt it, as I will be the sole voice of an enemy they cannot defeat. They will not be fool enough to threaten me. You will act as my transport and proof of the elementals' intelligence *and* benevolence. As the only threat to a titan Arsalia has to offer, it would be a great show of magnanimity that they have not only spared your lives, but released you and Squiggles. We will go to them with an offer of peace. They will have the option of allowing me to speak to all of Arsalia's mages or continue a war they have no reason to believe they can win."

"Sounds dangerous," admits Alice, "but if it helps, then I'm in,"

Twinkaleni nods, "Excellent. Now, I *must* stress the importance of stealth in your rendezvous with Danahlia and your father. To all of Arsalia, it *must* appear that you are still missing for our plans to succeed. It is vital that this conflict continue it's masquerade as a war of steel and stone. To give any doubt would be detrimental to our chances of success."

"Got it," assures Alice, checking over Squiggles, "it shouldn't take more than a few days."

Twinkaleni smiles up at her, "Well then, do be careful, and hurry back."

Having an agreeable plan has Alice feeling better about things. The two share a hug before Alice mounts Squiggles and flies off into the cool night air.

Chapter 7
Plans

Alice first heads for the Chevell estate, it being closer than her home town further south. After landing Squiggles in the forest nearby, she places the white stone in the tree hollow to signal Danahlia that she's waiting. Danahlia had last said she would be a away for a time but surely she was back by now. Alice waits with the same mix of excitement and nervousness that always gripped her when she awaited her Liguna to find her. She goes over all the things she would say, of what was going on in the north, her part in it, Twinkaleni's of course, and what needed to happen next. She tries to predict what Danahlia will say and do, trying to come up with counters to help insure her love would remain from harm. The day passes.

It wasn't terribly uncommon for Danahlia to only manage to sneak off after sunset, so Alice continues her vigil. She tries to keep the thought from taking root, but can't deny that it's entirely possible that Danahlia hadn't returned from her previous arrangement yet, or was even called away again after it. She fights with herself, one part of her saying to wait longer while the other demands she do something. Once the tension becomes too great, the Tokala decides to head to the Chevell manor for answers.

The Chevell's home is surrounded by a high stone wall so Alice must make her way to the main gate. This early, the large metal gate remains closed but even before true sunrise the grounds keepers are hard at work maintaining the immaculate flower garden set before the massive mansion. Wearing a hooded cloak in an effort to keep her identity secret, Alice manages to call one over. They say the Chevell's are still in mourning and not accepting visitors. Alice asks who was being mourned and the groundskeeper informs her that Edward Chevell, Danahlia's husband, was killed in the northern conflict. She asks if Danahlia was there, but the man says that since their marriage was dissolved, she had left, likely back to Feoria. She presses, but the man only apologizes for not knowing more. Alice wishes desperately to know of Danahlia's whereabouts and she considers trying to get an audience with Edward's mother. The countess generally didn't travel due to her health, but Alice decides it would be best not to be seen by any noble who might spread word of her passing. She thanks the groundskeeper and hurries on her way.

When she reaches the pixie forest, it's again night. As she makes her way to the ruins the Dippleblacks are currently living among, she's met by her father. It's clear Squiggles' noisy landing has awoken him and Alice apologises.

Her father takes her into his strong arms and strokes her fur, "For so many years I've awoken only to have you disappear into my dreams. To be able to rub my eyes and see you're still here is a wonderous gift. Don't ever apologize for it."

Alice lets herself be held until her father asks how Danahlia is, commenting that she had been gone a long time this trip. Alice reveals why she had really left, showing him the letter Lowe had originally given her.

"They can't... but you're... a titan?!" Robert Dippleblack exclaims, reading over the letter, fear, anger, and shock competeing for dominance on his face, "How can...? But you're back. Is it over?"

Alice frowns, "Not, quite," and explains what had happened.

She tells him about joining the army against the elementals, about Lowe, and the battles she was in. She goes on to say how she was knocked from the sky to find the elementals are actually golems controlled by her old friend and her rebellious mages, even the titan. She tells him of Twinkaleni's struggle and what the Murin had said about the Blood War likely having been orchestrated by the Royal Council. How even if Alice had fought and won the war for Arsalia, she and Squiggles would only be used again and again by these same people who threatened their lives. She then tells him of how she planned to help Twinkaleni's cause and needed to take him some place safe so she could do so without worrying about what might happen to him.

Now sitting on a log around their fire pit, her father takes some time to process this before smiling, though his eyes remain concerned, "Arsalia is our home. You were born here. Your mother, was here. Are you sure you want to leave it on the hope that your friend can beat such odds?"

"I think what Twinkaleni is fighting for is what's right. I saw the children they take, just little kids getting torn from their parents. They don't have any choices," says Alice, remembering her time at the

Order's academy, "The lives they have now are forced on them. It's not right, and it's not fair. I don't know if they can win. But I know if Squigs and me help, they have a better chance."

Robert Dippleblack's smile remains though the concern in his gaze deepens, "Sounds like your minds made." He looks away shaking his head with a sigh, "You've done all your growing up without me." He takes in a deep breath and lets it out. When he looks back to her, his eyes glisten, "You've gone through so much, done so much. You became a woman without me," he lets out a little laugh, "a dragon rider no less. I never would have imagined that." He places a hand over Alice's, "I am so proud of how strong you've become, but I am so very terrified of losing you again."

Alice holds her father's hand, "You won't, Dad. Twinkaleni has a plan to stop the fighting."

Robert Dippleblack let's out another little, sorrowful laugh and grips his daughter's hand, "Your Murin friend seems resourceful, but one thing I've learned in this life is that plans don't always go the way we want them to. You don't need my consent, but I'm not going to sit someplace safe while my only daughter fights a war."

"But dad-" Alice starts though her father cuts her off.

"No. There was too much I never got to do with you. I know it's my fault but don't deny me this. I'm sure your friends' rebellion can find some use for an old soldier."

Unable to dissuaded him, Alice and her father prepare for their journey. As they ascend on Squiggles, Alice considers which way to go. North back to Twinkaleni or west to search for Danahlia. Twinkaleni would prefer she return as soon as possible to reduce the chances of being spotted, but Alice desperately wants to see Danahlia and tell her what's going on. She consults with her father who says Danahlia is likely safe in Feoria but considering her standing she may be quickly remarried, which might place her back in Arsalia before Twinkaleni's rebellion can run it's course. Not liking the sound of that, Alice has Squiggles veer to the west toward Cold Blood territory.

Alice has Squiggles fly at top speed to take full advantage of the concealing night but before they can get very far, morning forces them to land. During the day, the three stay hidden in the largest forests they come across, keeping well away from settlements. They hunt, ride Squiggles as he hunts, and Alice tells her father of all Twinkaleni has accomplished already and what remains to be done, what the Murin hopes for the future and how she plans to make it happen. Having never met the mouse mage before, Alice can see that her father is none the less impressed with her.

A few night's flight has them in Feoria, and two more has Squiggles landing near Ter'Bour, the Cold Blood city Alice and her father were kept in during the last years of the Blood War. Ter'Bour is the capital of the territory known as Alorakarr, a land in which Javas Ashclaw is Dasan, or highest chief.

On their approach to the city, Alice and Robert Dippleblack are taken by guards, feeling it suspicious that Warm Bloods would be so far in Cold Blood territory, despite the end of the war. The guard captain they are brought before happens to be one of the warriors Robert Dippleblack had trained during their captivity and knows of the pair's standing with his chieftain. He hears them and escorts the Tokala to the great hall of Javas Ashclaw.

It wasn't the first time they had been but it is still impressive to see. The hall is more a fort than a home, being on a hill encased by thick stone walls dotted with towers. They walk up its single tight winding path that would be used to funnel any enemies foolish enough to challenge it. The Dippleblacks are brought to a room where they wait for Javas, but before the great chief can arrive, Danahlia bursts in.

No longer in a fancy dress but attired in the colorful clothes of her people, the Liguna exclaims, "Alice?! Rob?! What're you guys doin' here?"

Before either can respond, Danahlia grabs Alice in a hug, smothering the fox girl against her chest. After a moment, Alice manages to say, "We came lookin' for you after I heard you left the Chevell place."

"Yeah. Some crazy thing's happenin' up north in Arsalia, like a war or somethin'," Danahlia frowns, "Eddie got killed in it."

Alice hugs the lizard girl fiercely, "I heard, I'm so sorry, Danny."

After a moment, Danahlia looks to Robert Dippleblack, "You guys know what's happenin' over there? After we got the letter, they said I should go back to Feoria. Everything was so rush."

"Uh, yeah actually," says Alice, before explaining what was really going on.

Twink, our Twinkie, started a war?" Danahlia gasps.

Alice nods, "Sort of. She really wants to free the mages from the Order."

"Is she crazy?! How's she gonna fight a whole country?!" demands Danahlia.

"I've been wondering that myself," Alice's father admits, "But apparently she's already beaten back Arsalia's armies."

"She's usin' golems to fight and teaches the mages she frees to use 'em too," reveals Alice, "She found a rift in the mountains and can use it's power to even make a titan."

"A titan?! Like the thing we saw in the Wildlands?" asks Danahlia.

"Yeah, I haven't seen it but she says she used it to crush an entire army," says Alice.

Danahlia looks at her blankly for a moment, "Our Twinkie? Mini-mage? Big ears, no tail?"

"It's her. She even knocked Squigs and me outta the air with rocks, but it was all part of her plan. She's winning but only in the mountains. She needs help to free the other mages in the rest of Arsalia," Alice explains.

"Figures she'd need us. Let's go bail her out then," says Danahlia turning to head back the way she'd come.

Alice grabs the Liguna by the arm, "No, Danny, we want you to stay here in Feoria where it's safe."

Danahlia looks at her, shocked, "What? Are you kiddin' me? Twinkie's my friend too. I'm not gonna sit around like some Arsalian Lady, waitin' for another letter to tell me *you* died."

Danahlia turns again but Alice keeps her grip strong, "Danny, they might come after you to get to us. Twinkaleni and me are already in this. You don't have to be."

Danahlia laughs, "Ha, don't have to but gonna be. Do you have any idea how boring it is being a nobleman's wife? No way you're goin' adventurin' without me."

Before Alice can try to counter, Javas Ashclaw enters the room. He cocks a brow at his guests and smiles, "Both Dippleblacks have returned. Didn't get enough of my beautiful Ter'Bour the first time, eh?"

Javas takes them all to a dining room where they talk over food and drink. Alice explains all she knows of the conflict in Arsalia in as much detail as she can manage. The Cold Bloods were aware of something happening, if not precisely what, and Javas seems amused at the rival nation's troubles.

"This why we do not try to control the magic heya. We respect those who can touch neychah so. Arsalia pays because dhey do not."

"We gotta do somethin' to help," says

Danahlia, "Twinkie can't do this alone."

Javas shakes his head, "Feoria is tired of war.
The Dasan make it cleah we do not want more."
Before Danahlia can interrupt, the Liguna chieftain
holds up a finger, "But, taking magic from Arsalia's
armies would only benefit our people. I make no
promise of support, but I will speak with the Dasan.
I will tell dhem what you have told me."

"Thank you," says Alice sincerely, "We only
came to make sure Danahlia would be safe. Any
help you can provide will be greatly appreciated, I'm
sure."

"Whelp, mission failed, Furface," chimes
Danahlia, "'Cause I'm still comin' witcha."

"But, Danny-" Alice argues though Danahlia
cuts her off, rising from the cushion she sits on.

"Nope, this is happenin', make your peace with
it," calls back the Liguna as she races off.

Javas looks to Alice's father with a sigh and a
grin, "Ah, to be young and foolish again."

Unable to convince Danahlia to stay somewhere safe either, she, the Dippleblacks, and Squiggles head north. The Gadara Mountain range stretches over both Feoria and Arsalia. Alice uses it's thick forests to keep from being seen on her return to Twinkaleni and the rebels.

Well after crossing into Arsalia, Alice is considering where to land Squiggles as it's nearing sunrise. Before she can direct him to descend, her father alerts them to what looks like a star flying swiftly below and ahead of them. The white light is bright against the still dark forest and the group follows it curiously.

Alice is thinking it but Danahlia says, "Hey, that looks like one o' Twinkie's light balls." But then it disappears. Then two more appear, flying parallel to each other as if taking up the first one's cause.

"The mages must've spotted us. Maybe their guidin' us to Twinkaleni," suggests Alice, and she has Squiggles continue to follow the lights. The two lights soon disappear and three replace them, then four, then five. Feeling like she might recognize where she is, Alice says, "I think it means we're gettin' closer."

The lights vanish and Danahlia tells Alice to turn around. She has Squiggles make a U-turn and spots two lights swirling around one another heading straight up from an area they'd just passed. Figuring this was the mages signaling them, Alice has Squiggles land in a clearing nearby. When they touch down, they're greeted by a few of the young rebels and Twinkaleni.

"You brought them here?" asks the rebel leader in surprise.

"Hey, good to see you too, Twinkie," greets Danahlia, hopping down Squiggles' front leg. Some of the mages snicker.

"They want to help," says Alice, climbing off the dragon with her father.

After Twinkaleni greets Robert Dippleblack, she says, "A veteran with so many years of experience will certainly be an asset," she then looks to Danahlia, "But why have *you* come?"

Danahlia gasps, insulted, "Uh, *hey*, I happen to have all kinds of useful experience too!"

"I'm sure," Twinkaleni says with a raised brow, "I only wonder because Feoria would be a much safer place for you."

"Psh, like I'd miss this chance to see you," says Danahlia, grabbing Twinkaleni up easily and giving the Murin a squeeze. Twinkaleni squeaks indignantly and squirms until let loose.

While she takes a moment to straighten out her clothes and fur, the Murin mage admits, "I suppose it is good to see you as well."

Danahlia grins widely, then looks to all the young mages, "So, how we gonna clean up this mess o' yours?"

Twinkaleni explains to her new allies that after their latest defeat, the Arsalian army has remained on the defensive, having split into several large forces intent on defending their northern cities. She says her mages have been busy setting up defenses along the mountain's more traversable paths in an effort to prepare for another attack. Meanwhile, she has been anxiously awaiting Alice's return, eager to approach Arsalia's Royal Council while they still reel from their defeat.

As Alice and Twinkaleni make their plans and rehearse their stories, Robert Dippleblack takes to helping the mages prepare for battle by offering his knowledge of Arsalian military tactics. Danahlia has to be argued down from joining Alice and Twinkaleni, the two saying that her traveling with them would make it seem as if Feoria is allied with the elementals, which may be used as grounds to incite another war. Instead, Danahlia aids the mages with the survival skills she'd learned while in the mountains, much of which pertaining to acquiring food. Once they feel ready, Alice and Twinkaleni take Squiggles to Norwood.

They are right in suspecting the Arsalian army commander, Lord Alvaro, has placed himself and a substantial force there to protect the city and repair the damage done by Sven's team a few weeks prior. Alice is greeted by the Murin military leader and gives him the rehearsed version of what had happened to her and the loss of Lowe Fenris. She says she was taken captive by the elementals. During the time it took Squiggles to recover enough to fly, she had been reunited with her old friend, Twinkaleni.

Twinkaleni tells Alvaro that she made contact with the elementals while she was in the Gadara Mountains and claims they hail from further north in the Wildlands. Being magically gifted, she was able to communicate with them, telling them of herself and where she came from. Feeling some kinship with the Murin mage, they did not like the idea of those like her being imprisoned and used. The elementals collectively decided they would see the mages free and have since begun their campaign against Arsalia.

After finding the Warm Bloods to be far less resistant than they had anticipated, the elementals, convinced by Twinkaleni, now seek an alternative to spending the energy to destroy them. They have hence sent the Murin mage to negotiate her fellow magic wielders' release from bondage. The terms set by the elementals are: Arsalia will allow Twinkaleni to speak to her fellow mages, allowing them the choice of freedom, or Arsalia will be washed away under a tide of stone.

Surprised that they can communicate and shocked by the possibility of such an offensive, Alvaro wonders of Alice if the elementals do indeed have such power. Alice assures him that they number far greater than previously thought and only await the arrival of more titans meant to join them. She says they even released her and Squiggles to show their lack concern over Arsalia's strength. Alice and Twinkaleni express their urgency in reaching the Royal Council in Eledon, as the elementals will only wait so long before they assume Twinkaleni has been stopped in her mission and begin their attack. After trying and failing to get more information about this attack, Lord Alvaro gives them a detailed map of Arsalia and directions to help hurry them on their way. Alice and Twinkaleni head to the capital, elated that their story was so easily accepted.

It was not common knowledge yet that a dragon rider existed, and so Squiggles causes quite a commotion upon arriving in Arsalia's capital city. The guards that surround them hesitate to act, giving Alice a chance to explain themselves. After a time, the guard captain allows them entry on the condition that Squiggles wait outside the city walls. Eledon is by far the largest city Alice had ever been in and it takes time for their escort to get them to the castle at the city's center. A runner was sent ahead of them to bring word of their arrival, but they still have to wait sometime to be seen. While they do, they rehearse their story some more to prepare for their meeting with some of the most powerful people in Arsalia. Twinkaleni reminds Alice to leave as much of the talking to her as can be helped, knowing Alice to have a bit of a temper.

Eventually, they are allowed entry into a great and fairly empty hall of gray stone and expansive windows. Near the back end, up a few steps to insure it's above all others, is a massive throne. Fearsome, and possibly life size, lions act as arm rests for a seat clearly meant for someone particularly large. Though even these are dwarfed by the impressive metallic dragon, sitting just behind, acting as the throne's back so that one seated would be resting on it's well defined chest. The dragon's wings span protectively around the lions and their absent master. It's neck is hooked high, holding its ruby eyed head to look down imposingly at anyone standing before it. This dragon must be made to look like a different species, since it has very different facial features from Squiggles, more angular and spiked. The throne doesn't look overly comfortable but Alice figures comfort is not its purpose.

Before the throne are several lesser seats with tall backs arranged in a neat line. All face Alice and Twinkaleni but only the middle four are occupied. Elaborately clothed and seated are a white furred Lagomorph, an aged Leonain, a graying Rotan, and a robed Didel woman. The man escorting Alice and Twinkaleni introduces those seated before them as Lords Galvin, Aleser, Ferand, and Lady Huld. *So this is Lady Huld* Alice thinks, not overly impressed with the middle aged opossum woman.

Before their escort can announce them, the Rotan, Lord Ferand, welcomes, "Our dragon champion has returned."

The elderly Leonain, grumbles, "Champion? Champion of what? She and the Witchblood fell mere days into the failed offensive."

"You are unkind, Lord Aleser," interjects the Lagomorph, Lord Galvin, "You heard the reports. An ambush took our dragon rider from the sky," the rabbit man looks to Alice from the Leonain, "Most of us are pleased to see you well."

"Yes, though we are curious as to how," adds Lady Huld.

Alice gives her account of the battles she was involved in, how she was brought down by the elementals and saved by Twinkaleni despite having destroyed several of the earth creatures. The moment Twinkaleni's name is heard, the present members of the Royal Council react.

Most are subtle, but the Leonain, Lord Aleser, can't contain himself, "We have another traitor among us then, the rogue mage who aided in your attack on the Order in Klepor."

Alice decides she does not like the lion man and is about to spit something back but Twinkaleni puts a hand on her hip making her recall that the Murin insisted on being their speaker. Twinkaleni ignores the comment and shares her story of finding the elementals and telling them of how she had come to them.

"So, by your own admission, you have not only betrayed your Order, turned traitor to your own country, but have also poisoned the minds of these stone monsters against us!" bursts Lord Aleser.

"Many have already perished in the conflict

you have created," adds Lord Ferand.

"Execution would hardly fit the magnitude of such crimes," announces the Lagomorph, Lord Galvin.

"I wish to know more of these elementals," says Lady Huld, "You have their ear, you will arrange it so that we may meet with a representative. Let us see if we can stop the suffering you have caused Arsalia."

Twinkaleni looks sharply at the Leonain but manages to keep her voice even, "I, like all the magic wielders of Arsalia, was taken from my family, forced to use my abilities under threat of pain and death to become a weapon to be wielded by the likes of you. It is not I who have betrayed Arsalia, it is Arsalia who has betrayed me and all those with *real* power."

"How *dare* you!" Lord Aleser roars, standing from his chair, "I agree with Lord Galvin, death would be too lenient a thing for you. I will see your *suffer* for your treachery, *witch*!"

Twinkaleni ignores the lion man, instead

looking to Lady Huld, "*I* was chosen as the elemental's emissary, to relay their demands in a manner your kind would understa-"

"Demands?!" snarls Aleser.

Glossing over the lion lord's outburst, the Lagomorph wonders, "Our kind?"

"Those ungifted with magic," answers Twinkaleni blandly, "The elementals do not communicate with something as archaic as speech."

"Yet you have spoken with them?" asks the Rotan.

"Through the use of energy projection, similar to casting spells, I am able to make my thoughts and feelings known to them as they are able to do with me," says Twinkaleni.

"Are you saying only you can communicate with the elementals?" asks the Lagomorph.

"Convenient," grumbles the lion man, sitting back down.

"What of other mages then?" asks Lady Huld.

"Others can learn, though it is no simple task," answers Twinkaleni.

"You, dragon rider, do you confirm this?" growls Lord Aleser, his arms crossed.

"I've never heard them speak or have been able to talk to them," Alice admits honestly.

"What of the demands you spoke of?" asks Lord Galvin.

Twinkaleni nods, "It is clear Arsalia is not strong enough to defend itself from the elementals, especially not after the extended conflict with Feoria. The elementals are not primitive beings and I have explained to them the attachment mortals have to their physical bodies. Given that you will allow me to speak to all the mages of Arsalia and do not pursue those that choose to leave these lands, the elementals will discontinue aggression against your nation. Deny me this, detain me, or hinder my efforts to free my people, and they will destroy you all."

None seem happy with this and Lord Aleser rises again, "You vile little demon spawn! You think you can come *here* and make threats?!" He then looks to his counterparts, "I say we stretch the mageling. Make an example for all the tainted in Arsalia of what it means to defy order and civilization."

Deeply frowning, Lord Galvin, asks, "And what of the elemental threat?"

Aleser waves a hand vaguely north, "Let them come. They have strength in the mountains, but let us see what they can do in an open field against heavy cavalry. Let us see them try to roll rocks over us then!"

Angered by this man's ignorance and arrogance, Alice can't keep from barking, "They don't need to roll rocks to kill people!" The members of the Royal Council look to her as she goes on, letting the horrible memories of her battles fuel her words, "They can smash through men by the dozen with a swing of their arms. They can crush an Urock in full armor flat with a step. I know, *I've* seen it. So has Alvaro and every man who fought the elementals," she then looks directly at the Leonain,

"But *you* haven't. You haven't seen what they can do. It's no wonder you're so brave *now*," she waves her arms at the hall, "hiding here, so far away from the fighting."

"How *dare* you*!* You insolent little-," Aleser starts but is cut off by the Rotan.

"She has a point," says Lord Ferand loudly, then more calmly continues, "Your will would have use take many risks, Lord Aleser."

"All that has been proven is the elementals are not to be taken lightly. At the very least, we should bide our time until we can learn more," adds Lord Galvin.

Lady Huld asks Twinkaleni, "You had to explain to them the importance of our mortal bodies? What do you mean by this?"

Twinkaleni looks from Alice to the Didel, "From what I was given to understand, elementals are composed of magical energy, pure mana. They merely inhabit physical bodies to affect change in the world around them. The stone they encase themselves in is as armor and sword, as such, it can be discarded when damaged or no longer useful. The mana composing the elemental itself can then construct a new body. Essentially, they are immortal."

"Bold words," announces Lord Aleser, still standing, "I call their bluff. Alvaro mentions magic to be especially effective against these 'elementals.' They fear an Arsalia that wields magic against them. This is why they hide in the mountains, and this is why they want to take our mages. They have this little one thinking they only wish to help, but the moment we lose the ability to strike with sorcery, they will attack us, mark me."

The others consider this, looking for some kind of rebuke, but after a time, Lady Huld asks, "If we allowed your request, how do we know the elementals will not strike as Lord Aleser fears?"

"I fear nothing!" roars Aleser, becoming too riled up to contain himself.

"A poor choice of words, my apologies," Lady Huld is quick to say, giving a slight bow.

Then Twinkaleni answers the question, "You

do not. You mistake my purpose in coming before you. This is not a negotiation. *This* is an ultimatum."

Chapter 8
The Truth

Before Aleser can explode, Twinkaleni adds loudly, "But, if it brings you some comfort, from what they have expressed to me, they have no interest in Arsalia. If my wishes are kept, I intend to take those who would follow beyond Arsalia's borders and leave these lands for good. Once those who wish it are free, I will make it known to the elementals that there is no longer any need for violent force. No other lives need be lost."

"Are we to take the word of a traitor and merely hope for the best outcome?!" Aleser growls to the other council members, "If we give in to these monsters' demands we will appear weak. How long will it be then before Feoria comes to make demands of us as well?" The others consider and he adds, "We must fight to the last breath, with all our strength! To give any less would be the end of this kingdom."

"Whose last breath?" asks Alice, her eyes narrowed at the aged lion, "Yours or some poor soldier's forced to fight in your stead while you roar from within these walls?" Twinkaleni elbows Alice in the hip but she doesn't back down.

Aleser glares at Alice, taking a few steps down to her, "You question the strength of *my* courage, *girl*?"

"I'm sure she-" Twinkaleni starts, but Alice cuts her off.

"I don't question it's strength, *Lord* Aleser," says Alice, "I question it's very existence."

The rest of the council looks on with interest as Aleser comes to stand before Alice, a full foot and maybe more taller than she, "You talk of courage when you soar well above danger atop a dragon?"

Alice stands her ground, looking up into the furious man's eyes, "I fought against the elementals."

"Maybe you did," Aleser says, his words changing as his voice takes on a deadly edge, "And I've fought my share of enemies in my day, but not from atop a fearsome beast. I felt many a quivering lives stilled by my hands. I wonder how brave you are without your dragon. I wonder how much you'll talk without it's strength to carry you."

"Lord Aleser, I believe that is more than enough," Lord Galvin interjects.

"No, it's not," the Leonain calls back, though his glaring eyes never leave Alice's, "You overestimate your worth to us, dragon rider. You already failed against the elementals, and now it seems you sided with the enemy."

"Lord Aleser!" shouts Lord Ferand.

Aleser ignores him, calling back, "I believe we are no longer in need of the traitor's services. In which case, I shall take it upon myself to dispose of it."

"You would do so yourself, Lord Aleser?" questions Lady Huld, "Face the dragon rider, Alice Dippleblack, in a duel?"

Aleser smirks, still glaring at Alice, "A duel, tomorrow. We'll see what courage you have, girl, once I tear it from your guts and leave it spilled over the sands."

Alice narrows her eyes, fists clenched tight, "You're going to need more than words, my Lord. I hope your withered, old body can at least manage a modest fight."

Aleser sneers, turning away and the girls are escorted out.

The moment they exit the great hall, Twinkaleni looks over to Alice, "*That* was unnecessary. I had the situation well managed."

Still hot from the exchange, Alice spits back, "He hides in a castle and tells other to go fight in wars for him. He's a coward. I bet he's never fought a day in his life. Like you said, he thinks he's better than other people. I'm gonna prove 'im wrong."

Twinkaleni gives her head a disappointed shake, "You are a fool if you think he will face you himself. Those in seats of power are there specifically because they can get others to do their will for them. You will likely face a champion, a warrior of skill and strength chosen to face challengers such as yourself."

"But *he* challenged *me*!" Alice growls, her

anger at such a cowardly tactic bubbling over.

"You spoke against him, insulted him in front of the other council members. He seems a boisterous fool, but no one of influence should be taken lightly, it may only be an act."

Not willing to give voice to her growing apprehension, Alice states, "I'll beat 'im, and anyone he throws at me."

Twinkaleni sighs.

The girls spend the night with Squiggles and come the morning are escorted back into the city. This time they are taken to an arena, a large ring of wood and stone stands with a pit of sand in its center. More than a few people have come and Alice spots Lady Huld along with other members of the Royal Council in the best seats. Alice has her sword, Jellybane, but decides against wearing her armor. Twinkaleni questions the wisdom of this and Alice says she wants to be able to move freely. Lord Aleser, on the other hand, greets his opponent in a full suit of ornate plate armor that looks to be freshly polished to a mirror shine. Roaring golden lion heads decorate his breast plate, pauldrons, greaves, and even the helm crooked under one arm.

He grins at Alice's lack of protection, "Could you not even afford armor, peasant? At least think of those in attendance and try not to die too quickly."

"A shame your servant's work will go wasted when that shiny armor gets your blood all over it," Alice returns, keeping focus and ignoring the people around her. Aleser smirks and departs with a few men.

"I shall aid you but do be careful," says Twinkaleni.

Alice shakes her head, already a bit surprised that the Leonain planned to face her himself, "No, no magic. Only help if he cheats."

Twinkaleni looks to her as if for affirmation, "As you wish, but know, more lives than yours hing on your victory. Be alert, these people have no sense of honor. They only mean to win."

Alice nods and after a few minutes is parted from Twinkaleni. She is escorted through dark, unpleasant smelling halls under the stands to a large, closed gate.

Alice is nervous as she limbers up. She had never dueled anyone with the intent to kill before. Even with Aleser she only intended to humiliate, but to the lion lord this was clearly meant to be a fight to the death. Alice takes deep breaths and watches when her opponent is announced, his gate on the opposite side of the arena rising. Lord Aleser strides forth from the darkness, glittering brightly in the early sun. He wields a massive sword, easily twice the length of Jellybane. The weapon must be incredibly heavy but Aleser swings it around with apparent ease to the cheers of the crowd. Then she is announced as his challenger.

A loud voice calls her the dragon champion of Arsalia and her gate begins to rise. Once the gate is fully opened, Alice takes one more deep breath before stepping into the warm sun. The fighting pit is circular, large, and empty save for the two combatants. Immediately, Alice finds she doesn't like the pale sand that covers the ground. It feels too loose and uncertain under her feet but there was nothing she could do about it now. The gate behind her closes.

Alice doesn't make any show for the crowd, instead only holding Jellybane loosely at her side while keeping her breathing steady. She is perhaps thirty feet from Aleser and he takes steps toward her, perhaps thinking she will do the same to meet him in the center of the pit. She doesn't, choosing to remain where she stands knowing that each movement he makes under all that armor will only serve to tire him out. A short battle would be to her armored foe's advantage. She needed to draw it out.

He extends his heavy weapon to her in one hand, roaring, "Face me!"

His voice sounds more imposing coming from within his full helm. His highly polished armor catches the light and hurls it at her as well, making Alice squint to see past it. Alice doesn't like this either. Trying to look as calmly as she can, she walks further away to where the high surrounding stands still cast shadows. She leans her back against the smooth stone wall of the arena looking uninterestedly at the armored man.

The crowd begins to boo and Alice does what

she can to tune it out. They aren't important. Like her father had taught her, she keeps focus only on her opponent. Everything else is background. Aleser looks around at the crowd, many voices demanding that the two fight, before stamping after her. Once he's within a few paces he begins to charge, raising his weapon high over his head. Just before he brings the sword down atop her, Alice kicks off the wall, using the push to fling herself to Aleser's side and past him. His sword clangs loudly against stone and Alice swings for his back. But his sword is already there, having used some of his strike's momentum to circle around to meet her. Alice isn't ready for it and Jellybane goes flying from her grip. This close, Aleser has become a towering figure of steel that Alice no longer wants anything to do with. As he raises his blade for another splitting strike, Alice dashes away after her sword.

She reaches it but even as she shakes the sand loose, she hears Aleser clamoring just behind her. With speed she couldn't imagine the aged lion man possessing, he is already coming down with another cleaving strike. Alice is forced to drop Jellybane and leap backwards to avoid the attack that would have taken at least an arm. The sand absorbs some of her thrust and she doesn't get nearly as far as she had hoped. Aleser whips his sword around toward her to bring it up for a diagonal slash, but Alice is already scrambling away on her hands and knees. She gets to her feet and runs to the far end of the arena. Being so near death has Alice breathing hard and she struggles to regain her focus.

"At least die with dignity!" Aleser roars as he clangs after her.

The crowd boos and laughs at Alice's expense but she can see he is already slowing some in his movements. Alice hugs the wall as she circles around, trying to lead him away from Jellybane. When Aleser gets close, she takes to flinging handfuls of sand at his face, hoping to get some in the narrow eye slits of his helmet, before she darts away again. The sand is making her slow, but it hinders Aleser just as much and she is able to keep ahead of him. She also keeps him in the sun, knowing from her father that metal doesn't breathe. The sun isn't at it's fullest yet but it is rising, and with it, the temperature in Aleser's armor.

Alice taunts and baits him with easy access to her when he slows, getting him to use up more of his steadily draining energy. She dowses him with sand, forcing him to keep an arm up over his eye slits while he swings wildly with one handed sweeps of his blade. The length of the weapon means she must keep a safe distance away, but with each miss she is better able to judge his range and offer a more tempting target. He roars his anger, demanding that Alice stand and fight.

She calls back, "Fight you, my lord? But you haven't finished your grand battle with the air. It wouldn't be fair if I joined in."

Her antics begin to turn the crowd and some begin to laugh at the Leonain's anger. This only spurs him on, encouraging Alice to keep it up. She manages to retrieve Jellybane but still isn't sure how she can deal any real damage. His armor is well made and offers few weak points. Getting close enough to exploit them means getting in range of Aleser's greatsword, still being swung with speed and strength. Alice also has her own stamina to consider. Despite costing the Leonain with her maneuvers, she is needing to breathe harder and harder herself. She would need to end this soon or risk not having the agility to do so later.

While making these calculations, Aleser begins

to plod away, toward the remains of the shade at the very edge of the arena. He is booed for this and Alice calls after him, "Givin' up already?"

She can hear the exhaustion in his voice when he rumbles back without looking, "You are too cowardly to face me."

This was her chance. She dashes in, circling around to his back. The sand works in her favor now, muting her steps as she aims at one of the few chinks in his armor. The crowd gives her away though with its idiotic noises and Aleser brings his greatsword around in a wide slash just as Alice makes her lunge. She goes in low, aiming for the thin gap between plates behind his left knee. With all her weight behind the attack, her sword plunges deep. The lion lord roars in pain. Alice sees the shadow of Aleser's sword coming for her and she ducks as low as she can. It isn't enough.

Burning pain floods her senses causing her to yip and panic, loosing her balance to slip in the sand. Aleser tries to turn to her but with Jellybane stuck in his leg, the move only causes him more anguish and he collapses. Alice rolls away when he tries to reach for her, a horrible searing sensation coming from over one of her eyes. Once she's out of his reach she feels for it to find much of her right ear missing, only bloodied fur where it was. As the downed man shouts obscenities, Alice checks for anymore damage but finds it to be her only wound. Instinctively, she looks around for her ear but only sees blood and sand. Aleser is trying to get back to his feet and is too close to Jellybane for Alice to make a grab for it.

Her ear burns terribly but it isn't life threatening. A standing Aleser is. She pulls free her bone bladed knife and makes her way to the man, moving around to keep from his line of sight. He tries to brace himself with his greatsword, but only fumbles back to the ground, showing that his left leg is completely useless. Knowing her knife couldn't pierce his armor, Alice leaps atop Aleser's back, forcing him face first into the sand. She yanks off his helmet to reveal a much thicker and darker mane than the aged lion man's. The crowd takes in a surprised breath and Alice puts her knife to the man's throat, forcefully turning his head so she could see that it was a much younger Leonain.

"I yield, I yield," he breathlessly begs as Alice presses the knife against his jugular.

"Who are you?" Alice demands, "Where's Aleser?"

The man says nothing, his yellow eyes wide in fear. The crowd begins to voice its anger at being duped. Alice lets the man go, recovers Jellybane, and calls out to the arena, "You are truly a coward, Lord Aleser! You challenge *me* to a duel and then can't even find the courage to show yourself?"

The crowd shares its disapproval of the Leonain's absence and Twinkaleni's voice shouts from the stands, some magic lending it strength, "Are these the hands that should guide Arsalia?! Ones quick enough to direct others to war and death as long as they can stay safe behind their servants and high walls?!"

Tired, Alice lets her pain fuel her fury as she commands, "Come out, Aleser! Claim whatever shreds of dignity you still can or I will hunt you down and drag you from whatever hole you've crawled into!" After a few breaths and still no response, she mocks, "My dragon has never had lion before, though I guess he'll have to settle for quivering kitten!"

The gate the armored man stepped from reopens. Seething with rage, Aleser bursts from the darkness with longsword in hand. He is unarmored, wearing a simple drab cloak.

He swiftly closes the distance between them roaring, "How dare you speak to me you filthy little peasant! Do you have any idea who I am?! My blood is that of kings! A single breath is too precious to be wasted on garbage like you! To soil myself by even holding a weapon to such low born scum!"

Alice readies her sword as the man approaches, mad with anger.

"I'll have you tortured long for this. I'll have your family tortured. I'll have your whole damn village tortured!" Aleser shouts as he raises his sword high over his head.

Alice sneers, "But my Lord, you're missing something."

"What?!" Aleser barks back, holding his strike for a moment.

"Your FOOT!" Alice shouts, leaping forward.

Aleser brings his blade crashing down but only hits sand.

Alice dodges to his side and swings Jellybane with both hands. The enchanted blade cuts low on Aleser's shin. He howls in pain, falling forward, his right foot left standing as Aleser holds on to his leg, shocked and outraged that he could even be experiencing pain.

He falls near the man Alice had dueled and demands through his anguish, "Kill her *now* you worthless idiot!"

"My lord, I can't, my leg..." the man confesses, grimacing and gesturing to his maimed limb.

Aleser pulls a dagger from somewhere on his person and stabs the other man in the neck. The crowd gasps in surprise as the man burbles wetly, eyes wide at the fallen lord.

Aleser pulls free the dagger, sending blood spilling in a small arc and snarls, "Surrounded by idiots," then to the crowd he shouts, pointing vaguely to Alice, "She is a traitor to the realm! A thousand glints for her head!"

"Alice Dippleblack fought honorably, though this member of the Royal Council did not!" shouts Twinkaleni.

"*Former* member of the Royal Council," calls Lady Huld from the stands. She looks to Alice, "Do Arsalia justice and rid us all of this dishonorable, *murderous* fool."

If she didn't know it before, she knew it now, Aleser is a murderer. He's just like the monsters Twinkaleni described these social elites to be. The moment the armored warrior was no longer of use, Aleser killed him without a second thought. He even plainly said he would pay to have Alice herself killed. He cheated in the duel *he* challenged *her* to. Lord Aleser, member of the Royal Council, was a truly despicable man. She now had the opportunity to rid the world of him.

Alice looks down at the disgraceful Leonain, blood soaking into the sand from his injury. She looms over him, pointing her sword at his chest, asking loud enough so only he would hear, "Did you and the Royal Council start the Blood War?"

Aleser, having abandoned his dagger in favor of desperately trying to stem the blood flowing from his leg, slaps at Jellybane, snarling, "Don't dare point that thing at me, scum!"

With a swift thrust Alice catches Aleser's slapping hand on Jellybane's point and pins it to the ground. Aleser screams and she asks again more sternly, "Did you and the Royal Council start the Blood War?"

"Finish him!" Lady Huld commands from the stands.

The lion lord spits, "Kill me and you and your filthy wretch of a father will die! Burned both of you!"

Alice twists her sword, forcing the bones of Aleser's hand to spread unnaturally. Aleser cries out in agony and Alice asks once more, "Did you and the Royal Council start the Blood War?"

When Aleser isn't forth coming, Alice twists

Jellybane some more, getting more screams from the noble, "This is your only chance at life, *my lord*. Answer honestly and I will leave you to lick your wounds. Don't and-" Aleser screams again as Alice continues twisting her blade.

"WE HAD TO!" Aleser confesses mid scream. Alice stops. "We had no choice. It would have been civil war," Aleser whimpers.

Alice looks down in disgust at the man who had contributed to a war that had cost so many lives, including her mother's. "You deserve to die," says Alice, her voice suddenly breaking and vision blurring, "For all you've done, you deserve it."

"You wretched whore, you said you would spare me," snarls Aleser through his pain.

Jellybane's blade begins to glow attracting Alice and Aleser's attention. The enchanted weapon flares brightly for a moment before Aleser's thumb, fore, and middle fingers drop off his hand, neatly cleaved off by the sword's magic. Upon seeing this, Aleser begins to scream once more, displaying an impressive array of obscenities. Jellybane, now free of any stains, is returned to it's sheath as Alice turns away from the cursing lord.

His voice stops abruptly and Alice turns back to see Aleser shaking violently, his hands clutching desperately at the sand just before becoming rigid. Blood begins to leak from his nose and eyes. Uncertain of what just happened, Alice then feels something she hadn't in a long time, her body becoming light as air. She begins to float. The shocked crowd gasps and points to her while she is lifted away from the crimson stained sand and comes to a soft landing beside Twinkaleni in the stands.

Someone announces, "The, the victor, Alice Dippleblack, dragon champion of Arsalia!"

Few cheer, though most only look in shock. A warrior was murdered, a Royal Council member lay slain, and a young woman flew. The observers nearest Alice and Twinkaleni step away as the rest of the crowd begins to murmur.

Alice, suddenly feeling very tired, reaches for her still stinging ear. Twinkaleni has her kneel down so she can check it.

"How's it look?" Alice asks, breathing deeply and leaning her head to one side.

"Grisly, but I do not believe your life is in immediate danger," says Twinkaleni, "Nonetheless, we should locate a healer immediately."

"That will not be necessary," comes Lady Huld's voice, the Didel approaching them from the parting crowd. She waves to an older Houdain dressed in colorful robes following her, "Gifre, tend to our champion."

Alice and Twinkaleni look warily at the dog man and he lifts his hands revealing he holds a container and cloth, "I am a healer of some repute. Most would be grateful to be attended to by one of my experience." When the young women do not drop their guard, he adds a bit softer, "The wound may fester if left untreated."

Alice lets him near and be pours a bit of water on his cloth to clean her ear, Twinkaleni watching closely. Wincing as he does, Alice wonders, "Will it grow back?"

"Afraid even I do not have such power. All that

can be done is to seal the wound. Now, hold still."
After the man tosses away the damp cloth, he
begins making gestures over Alice's head. As he
does, she can feel the burning in her ear soothed to
a warmth. After a few more moments, the warmth
ends and he hands the water bottle to Alice before
moving to retake his place behind Huld.

Twinkaleni stands on her toes to see, "How is
it?"

Alice feels around her ear. It doesn't hurt
anymore, but it was definitely gone. "Ok, I guess,"
she replies, then to the healer says, "Thanks."

Lady Huld gives the man the slightest bow as
he passes, "Thank you, Gifre."

Gifre bows lower, "By your will, my lady."

"You have done a great service for Arsalia by
removing that lying, cowardly, pompous, excuse for
a man," Huld assures Alice, "If you would
accompany me, I believe we have a great deal to
discuss."

For several days, Alice and Twinkaleni are

asked to meetings with the remaining members of the Royal Council as they "try to understand the situation and determine the course that will do the most good for Arsalia." The pair are asked many probing questions about their stories and the elementals. Despite this, Twinkaleni manages to come up with swift responses that, if she didn't know better, would be convincing even to Alice.

When asked why the elementals have any interest in seeing the mages free, Twinkaleni responds that they feel a kinship with the mages. Both house mana within themselves, unique to other life. A difference though is that the elementals do not create their own mana and thus tend to stay near sources rich with it. As they have discovered, mages not only generate mana within themselves, but can even use their power to infuse the elementals with it, making it possible to leave their mana rich homes for extended periods. This is a gift the elementals desire greatly and will see Arsalia's mages freed to gain it.

The Council wonders if this would not simply make the mages servants of the elementals. Twinkaleni says it will not, that theirs will be an alliance of mutual benefits. The Murin mage expresses her plans to leave Arsalia and begin a new community beyond it's borders. Here the, mages will live in harmony with the elementals, exchanging their freedom granting power for the elementals' guardianship.

Lord Galvin asks, "You would leave Arsalia with your band of rogue mages? What assurance do we have that you will not simply muster a greater force and attack us again with your call to 'liberate' your people?"

"I and the elementals will leave Arsalia with those who would follow me. *You* will insure I do not decide to strike again by disbanding the Order of Thermathrogi indefinitely."

More Royal Council members had begun to attend these meetings and all express their displeasure.

An old Echanian lord claims, "The Order of Thermathrogi has been in loyal service for hundreds of years. Such an institution is not so easily dissolved."

The others agree and the Rotan, Lord Ferand

says, "The Order is needed for Arsalia's very survival. The mages it produces provide much needed strength to our armies. Respectably, you seem to at least be searching for nonviolent means to attain your goals. I'm sure you would understand that a strong army negates the need for violence simply by standing. Removing such strength would weaken the army as a deterrent for war."

Twinkaleni nods, "I understand your concerns. The current Order *will* disband, this is not negotiable, but any mages choosing to remain loyal to Arsalia will be free to train as the weapons you so wish them to be. My aim in removing the Order is to prevent the magically gifted from being forced into servitude, taken as children from their families, likely never to see them again, to be beaten and tormented, to be indoctrinated and forged into mindless machines of death as I was meant to be. As my compatriots were meant to be. And as is happening at this very moment to hundreds of others unheard within the walls of every *one* of the Order's vile academies."

Twinkaleni's voice has risen to such intensity that the Council is left silent for once. Even Alice looks down to the Murin at her side to insure she remains half the Tokala's height.

Eventually Lady Huld asks, "And after providing transportation to the 'liberated' mages, do *you* intend to stay in Arsalia, Alice Dippleblack?"

"No, I and my dragon will follow the mages into the Wildlands to ensure their safety," Alice says firmly and sees Twinkaleni look up at her from the corner of her eye.

"This is rather disappointing to hear," says Lord Ferand, "If we were to lose some mages but retain our dragon champion, this would give us some balance, but to lose both..."

The others Council members murmur words like unacceptable and unreasonable.

Over this, the old horse lord announces, "Perhaps some change *is* needed. I have not spent a great deal of time in the academies of the Order, and this news of beating and tormenting is new to me. Are you certain it is not isolated?"

"It is not," affirms Twinkaleni, "the mages that I have already liberated confirm this. And many of those who do not seek freedom do so only because they fear the repercussion of even daring to hold the thought."

"If," starts Lord Galvin, "the conditions were to improve for the mages under the Order's care, would it be agreeable then for it to remain in service?"

"Perhaps even a representative of yours might make inspections of a sort to assure this," offers Lord Ferand.

"If this were to even be considered, a condition would remain that a mage would choose to attend the academy and must be free to leave if they wish without reprisal," says Twinkaleni.

The Council seems slightly more agreeable to this and after a bit more deliberation the meeting is over.

Lady Huld will often seek to speak with Alice individually, generally to confirm parts of Twinkaleni's stories. She claims she does what she believes is in Arsalia's best interest and more or less apologizes for any hint of threat in her letter, saying it was only to stress the urgency of the situation. Huld also makes promises of great reward for Alice's aid in nullifying the elemental threat, mentioning land, wealth, and comfort not only for her but any children she might have. Alice does her best to keep to Twinkaleni's story even when Huld mentions her dragon's fire destroying the elementals and wonders if regular fire is as effective. Alice tells her that dragon fire is special in that it burns away the magic animating the elementals while regular fire does not, stressing that further conflict with the earth and magic born creatures would only result in more Arsalian lives lost.

After their last meeting, Alice and Twinkaleni are called once more. This time they are told that the Royal Council will allow Twinkaleni to speak to the mages in the academies across Arsalia under the condition that a representative from each is present. Twinkaleni agrees as long as the representative is not allowed to interrupt and is only present to listen. An arrangement reached, the Council says it will have documents written in the next days to show Twinkaleni has it's authority to continue her mission. The Murin mage counters by producing her own parchment stating this. She adds the amendments and then says she only requires the signatures of each member to continue. She shows it to the Council and it is read aloud. After a few moments of discussion, the Council is unable to find fault with it and concedes to sign.

Once she has it, Twinkaleni expresses her desire to leave the capital immediately. When Alice asks why, the small mage says that it is likely the Council will send messengers out to all of the Order with instructions to poison the minds of the mages they hold against her. This will make it that much more difficult to convince them to leave and seek lives of freedom. With the map they received from Lord Alvaro, Twinkaleni plots a course that will take them to major cities in the south. With southern Arsalia being farthest from the mountains, getting to those mages first is critical since if Arsalia becomes hostile toward them, they will not likely have another chance.

As has been the case since shortly after they had arrived, a crowd surrounds Squiggles, who waits just outside Eledon in a nearby field. The curious onlookers are kept back by guards stationed around the dragon. Squiggles doesn't seem to mind the gawkers much, as some throw him bits of food. When Alice and Twinkaleni approach, they are assaulted with questions about the great reptile. Not wishing to waste time, the pair ignore them the best they can, mount up, and head south to their first academy.

Chapter 9
Freedom

On their way south, Twinkaleni has Alice fly over as many large cities as they can. They search for the unique block like structure that would indicate an academy but find none until they enter Arsalia's southern territories. When they spot one in Dacia, the Order's academy building looks very much like the one in Klepor, even having a walled yard around the entire thing. Alice has Squiggles land here, much to the surprise of the guards, who's torches show them retreating into the safety of the academy. Alice and Twinkaleni knock on the main door and have to talk through it to convince the frightened guards of the purpose of their visit. Even this late in the evening, Twinkaleni demands that the grand master of the academy be brought before her immediately.

After a few minutes' wait, an elderly Mustaroni swings open the door shouting, "What is the meaning of this?! How dare you de-"

He freezes, his words catching in his throat, when Squiggles lowers his massive head to look at the tiny weasel man before him. Squiggles grumbles his hunger and the wide eyed grand master jumps, falling backward.

"I am hear to speak to the mages of this academy," says Twinkaleni, holding out her signed document, "You will see to it that they are brought to the northern gates by morning's first light. Do you understand?"

The man has to be told several more times, his mind too stunned by the dragon's presence to comprehend words. Eventually he gets it and agrees to do as he is bid, seeing the signatures of the Royal Council. Alice is grateful when he closes the door. She's fairly sure he soiled himself. The pair take Squiggles to a nearby forest so he can find something to sate the rumble in his belly. Before morning, the pair return to Dacia's northern gate to await the mages' arrival.

Alice, becoming bored and curious, wanders around just inside the city while Twinkaleni waits patiently with Squiggles. She spots the mages in their drab robes being escorted by several guards and what Alice presumes is one of the Order's masters. The mages range from small children to young adults. The youngest of them are huddled together, looking nervously around at the people watching the strange procession. Alice knows this is likely because the mages were taught to fear the persecution of 'normal' people. This was paired with the teaching that their powers were given to them by demons, which would make them 'justifiably' despised by the public and could even provoke violence. Only after they had mastered their powers and the demons within could they be trusted to leave their academies, and only then, to serve Arsalia. This is why Twinkaleni wanted them to come to the gate, not only out of their academy but outside the city walls. Her first demonstration of the lies told to them by the Order.

Alice hurries to rejoin Twinkaleni and Squiggles. She is amused to see the first mages and their guards freeze upon seeing the dozing dragon, then to be bumped into by those behind them. Twinkaleni goes to greet them warmly, assuaging their initial fears, and to introduce herself along with her purpose. She touches each of them, perhaps more than fifty in all, letting them feel her aura, telling them that she too is a mage who was once imprisoned as they were. While she shares her story with them, she introduces Alice and Squiggles. Alice mostly listens and helps those who want to approach the lazily resting dragon. She does however aid in countering some of the accusations thrown at Twinkaleni, mostly from the older, more heavily indoctrinated mages.

The mages are told of the Order's lies and long history of enslaving the magically gifted for use by Arsalia. After a time, the attending master bursts, going as far as calling Twinkaleni a blasphemer and leader of demons. Twinkaleni uses this to force the man to leave, as it was the Royal Councils agreement that an Order representative could only attend if they remained silent. Slowly, over many hours, Twinkaleni removes obstacle after obstacle, barrier after barrier instilled in the mages by the Order of Thermathrogi.

Knowing there may be spies among them, Twinkaleni keeps to the story of the elementals aiding the mages. This way, if the Royal Council gets wind of her speech, the secret behind the war of steel and stone remains hidden. She tells the mages of her plans to leave Arsalia for good and begin a new community free of oppression, one where they can bring their families and live together again. This seems to appeal greatly to the younger mages who still have the luxury of remembering their families.

Some wonder if they can simply go home rather than leave Arsalia. Twinkaleni says that she will not stop them, but even if they do, she cannot guarantee that the Order will not seek to take them once more.

She speaks to the mages for two days, then on the third they are asked to come only if they have decided to leave the Order. Twinkaleni is pleased to see over a dozen wish to leave, though it turns out that most simply want to return to their homes. Alice and Twinkaleni decide to aid them in this, acquiring documents stating where the young mages were taken from the masters of Thermathrogi. Having been hopeful of their success, Twinkaleni had Squiggles fitted with a heavily looped, net like mesh to go across his back to offer handholds for any liberated mages. With those departing on board, they take to the air.

The mages who lived far from Dacia are dropped off in their various towns and villages. Once on the ground, the mages give their farewells to their friends and thanks to Squiggles, Alice, and Twinkaleni. By the time they have dropped off all that wanted to go back to their homes, only four remain to join Twinkaleni's rebellion. Feeling they are too few to worry about going all the way back to the Gadara Mountains, Twinkaleni decides she wants to try another academy, then another. Once they gather enough, Alice flies Squiggles back to the mountains to drop them off. There they are told the full truth of the elementals being golems and the rebellion grows.

Alice and Twinkaleni work their way across Arsalia, taking 'the most efficient' route. Each academy sees mages liberated and a handful more who decide to leave Arsalia behind. It is revealed that Twinkaleni was right in that the Royal Council would send instruction to the Order to warn the mages against her. They find this out when a young mage, told not to speak of it, wonders if Twinkaleni is really a demon in disguise, unconvinced by the Murin's diminutive stature and harmless appearance. Prepared for such propaganda, Twinkaleni gives them her speech of how their powers are not the result of a demonic presence within them, lurking about, waiting to take over the moment they loose control. She even shows them her mastery over the 'mana fury' state in which her eyes emit their golden glow. Time and time again, she uncovers the Order's lies, convincing more and more mages of the truth.

When Alice and Twinkaleni are dropping off another dozen or so newly freed mages in the Gadara Mountains, they hear from the others that a bat rider of Feoria came with news. The rider had said that the Cold Bloods were moving to support the rebel mages' cause. An army of many hundreds under Javas Ashclaw and several other chieftains is gathering along the border territories. It is stressed that this force will not engage Arsalia and is only meant to divert attention to itself in an effort to keep the Warm Bloods distracted. Now with Feoria's support and steadily more mages joining, or at least leaving the Order, it looked like Twinkaleni's rebellion is well under way. That is until one day, upon another return to the mountains, Alice spots something strange ahead.

"Is that fog?" she wonders aloud, shielding her eyes against the lowering sun. Fall was only just setting in and the weather had been dry.

Twinkaleni peers from around her, "It seems an odd time for it."

As Squiggles flies into the approaching cloud spanning the horizon, Alice opens her mouth, expecting a cool refreshing mist, but instead is hit with an acrid taste and odor that stings her eyes and dries her tongue.

"Ugh, it's smoke!" Alice spits, having Squiggles fly higher to get above it.

"I wonder what burns? Only an immense fire could, be..." Twinkaleni trails off before shouting, "The mountains! We must reach them at all haste!"

A horrible feeling grips Alice's stomach as she calls for the mages with them to hold on, bringing Squiggles to full speed. The smoke gets steadily thicker as they head north and before long they find the source. Even at this distance and through the thick haze, they can make out a bright wall of flame. The Gadara Mountains are on fire.

As they near, Alice can see what must be the Arsalian army. They are thinly spread below with wide trenches dug before them and stand well away from the raging fires consuming the thick forest covering the mountains.

"Fools!" Twinkaleni curses, "They have finally called our bluff!"

Alice has Squiggles race to the mages' primary caves, well above the fire line but still mired in thick smoke. They land quickly and are met by Danahlia and a few of the older mages.

"Alice!" the Liguna calls out, running to them, "It's about time you guys got here! The whole mountain's goin' up! Come on, come on, come on!"

"What happened? Where is everybody?" Alice asks, leaping off Squiggles to help the newest rebels down, startled even more at seeing a Cold Blood.

Twinkaleni lessens the gravity around them with her magic allowing for easy dismounting as she asks, "Has everyone evacuated?"

Danahlia takes the frightened mages, guiding them to the ground, "Most already went through but Sven and some of the others at the further camps hadn't made it back yet," she looks to Alice, "Your dads still out there too."

"What? Where?!" Alice asks, lowering the last of the mages.

"He said he was goin' to look for any stragglers," Danahlia replies, "That was a few hours ago when the smoke started buildin'. The watchers near the foot saw the army gatherin' and diggin' trenches. They came back when the fires started gettin' lit. We been taken groups through the tunnels to the other side ever since."

Twinkaleni had chosen this spot as the mage's main camp specifically because it had the shortest tunnel that led all the way through the mountains and to the Wildlands on the other side. She had the evacuation route planned encase they were ever overwhelmed by Arsalia's army but didn't consider the possibility of using it to escape an inferno.

"Have the scouts been released?" Twinkaleni asks. One of the mages says they were. Any Arsalian scouts the mages found were captured if possible and had been kept within the caves. Now abandoning the mountains, they would have no use in keeping them.

As Alice is climbing back aboard Squiggles to look for her father and the other mages, Robert Dippleblack walks into the clearing. His fur, usually bright orange, is faded with ash. In his arms is a particularly young, mageling girl, and limping beside him is Lowe Fenris.

"Dad! Lowe!" Alice cries, leaping back off the dragon to rush to the quickly surrounded trio.

"Lady, Dippleblack," Lowe grins weakly, his body practically hanging off her father.

"Lowe, what happened? I thought you were dead," gasps Alice, draping the Lobovan's arm over her shoulder.

Lowe winces as his weight is transferred. "Not quite, it seems..." he rasps, then leans so heavily onto Alice that she can't tell if he's still conscious.

Robert Dippleblack explains that he had found them trying to make their way to the caves. Elodie, the young Leeseran mageling, had found Lowe barely clinging to life after falling from Squiggles and nearly being crushed to death under rocks. She had hidden and tended to him the best she could in secret for fear of Twinkaleni being angry with her for aiding an Arsalian soldier. The squirrel girl cries, apologizing profusely for her deceit.

"You have nothing to apologize for, Elodie. Were the ungifted of Arsalia as caring as you to we mages, none of this would have ever needed occur," assures Twinkaleni, then to one of the older mages, she says, "Take them through. The rest-"

Heavy thumping and breaking branches has everyone cautiously looking to the trees. A few seconds later, several oddly shaped golems crash through the brush into the clearing. They walk on four legs like ferals and have very wide, bulbous bodies. The front ends of these crumble away to reveal handfuls of mages held within. They scramble forth to join the others already assembled. The last to get off the rock creatures are Sven and a few of the other more senior mages. Once they step free, their golems collapse into rubble.

"Sven!" calls Twinkaleni, scampering over to him.

"Twinkaleni!" coughs Sven, "You've made it! Arsalia has ignited the mountains! They mean to smoke us out or see us all taken by flames!"

"I've seen them. Is this everyone?" asks Twinkaleni, looking over her people.

"I believe so," replies Sven, "We've gathered all from the caves to the west. Those to the east should already be through."

"Excellent. Have you any strength left?" wonders Twinkaleni.

Sven stands a little straighter, "Of course."

Twinkaleni smirks and announces, "Then, all those with proficiency in fire and earth come with me. We are to gather as many earth stones as we can and collapse the other caves that lead through the mountains. The rest, take to the main tunnel. We will meet you on the other side once our work is done."

As the mages split into two groups, the majority heading into the cave, Sven wonders, "You intend to raise the titan?"

"I intend to make Arsalia regret all they have done to us," says Twinkaleni, then to those on her team she announces, "If we do not make a show of force now, the army may be tempted to follow us to the Wildlands," she turns to Alice, "We need time to prepare. They will not likely strike until dawn, letting the fires do their work, but if they do, can we count on you to deter them?"

"Uh, yeah, of course," says Alice, not entirely sure what she might do.

"You can count on *us*!" affirms Danahlia.

Alice starts, "Danny, you shou-"

"No way you're gettin' to be the hero all by yourself," Danahlia crosses her arms, "I'm comin'."

Knowing better than to argue with the stubborn Liguna, Alice concedes, "Fine, we need to get Lowe to the army anyway. They'll have healers."

Danahlia cocks a brow, "The army? Aren't they the ones tryin' to kill us?"

"Lowe needs a healer. They're closest. Besides, he's one of 'em," says Alice, her father helping her get the wounded Lobovan to Squiggles. Twinkaleni then has him floated up atop the dragon.

As Danahlia and Alice climb into place, Robert

Dippleblack decides, "I'm coming too."

Alice holds a hand to him, "No, Dad, it'll be too dangerous."

"Which is exactly why you'll need me," her father counters.

"Dad, if things go bad and Squigs has to fight, you could fall off. I almost lost Lowe last time, I won't risk losing you." He opens his mouth but Alice continues, "We've been ridin' Squigs since he could fly, we know how he moves. Besides, you have more survival experience than anyone. The mages need you. Help them, for me."

Her father frowns and Alice can see the various responses he wants to give in his eyes, but then he settles on a hug, saying, "Be careful."

Alice hugs him fiercely and Twinkaleni calls, "We have our tasks," then to those going into the caves she says, "If we do not arrive by midday, collapse the tunnel and proceed without us. I wish you all good fortune."

The groups break and Squiggles takes to the

air.

Ascending through the choking smoke, Alice feels Danahlia shifting Lowe around behind her, grumbling, "Ticks, he's heavy. Who is this guy anyway?"

Alice tells her of Lowe Fenris and how he ended up in the state he was in on their way down to the Arsalian army gathered near the foot of the mountains.

Lowe puts a weak hand on Alice's shoulder, "I wish, to remain by your side, my lady."

Alice half turns to him, "What?"

"I was meant, to be your shield, allow me to..." Lowe's hand slips off, the effort taking too much out of him.

Instead of answering Alice has Squiggles dive low before Arsalia's lines. She ignores the shouts of the assembled men, searching for Lord Alvaro's banner while describing it to Danahlia. After one pass and not seeing it, she has Squiggles turn around for another, this time landing just before the center battalion. Men rush forth to form a semicircle around Squiggles, weapons lifted. The dragon grumbles his warning and the men keep their distance. A few on horseback approach. She recognizes the Bovidan in the lead from Alvaro's meetings but can't recall his name.

"What is the meaning of this?" he bellows.

"Where's Alvaro?" asks Alice.

"*I* am in command here. Now state your business."

"We found Lowe Fenris," says Alice, "He was thought lost but has been recovered. He needs a healer."

The bull man considers for a moment before jerking his horned head at a few men who then tentatively approach. The Bovidan calls for someone named Sedrick to be brought. He then asks, as Danahlia helps position Lowe to be taken by the men, "Does this mean you've come to your senses and intend to fight with us once more, dragon rider?"

"No, but I did come to warn you," says Alice, then raises her voice for all to hear, "The elementals are furious for what you've done! They're sending a titan to destroy you! I suggest you run while you can!"

"HA!" the Bovidan mocks, "We know the truth of it. The stone men fear us. This is why they hide in the mountains. There are no titans!"

Alice is about to say more but Lowe grabs her hand as he's being taken by the men, "My lady, allow me to stay by your side."

Alice smirks down at him, his hand slipping away from hers, "You're no use to me like this. Get better, then come find me."

As he's being taken away he shouts with whatever strength he has left, "I will! I will find you! I will earn my kiss!"

The Bovidan raises a brow at Lowe as he's taken behind the lines and then turns back to Alice, "By morning, the fires will have scorched much of the mountains. There will be nowhere left for the stone men and their pet mages to hide. Stand against us then and we will destroy you too."

"You can't beat them," Alice spits back, "All you're doing is taking more husbands, fathers, and sons from Arsalia! Let the mages go!"

"ENOUGH!" the bull man bellows, raising a ringed finger to Alice. The men present raise their weapons and Squiggles snarls his agitation, spreading his wings threateningly. This startles the Bovidan into shouting, "Rairak!"

The ring on his extended finger glows an azure blue just before a thin bolt of lightning arcs from it, hitting Squiggles in the neck. The dragon recoils, roaring his outrage. Alice and Danahlia feel the snap of electricity. It causes them to cry out though more in surprise than pain. Squiggles recovers quickly, turning his massive head to bare his many sharp teeth at the bull commander, an angry rumble in his throat. Shocked into stillness by the magical blow's lack of effect on the giant reptile, the soldiers watch as the Bovidan nervously points his finger again, this time at Squiggles' face. Just as his mouth opens to form the word once more, Squiggles lunges forth, snapping his powerful jaws over the bull man and his horse. The poor equines cries out as it and it's master are taken skyward to be wetly crunched and swallowed.

It takes a moment to process before someone yells, "ATTACK!"

Shouting their anger, the army rushes forward launching more bolts of lighting, fire balls, and spears. Alice and Danahlia press their bodies against Squiggles, screaming for the dragon to fly. Enraged, Squiggles unleashes a deafening roar at the tiny figures before him, halting their charge. The air trembles with the dragon's fury and Alice can see some men fall to their knees, dropping their weapons to cover their ears. Squiggles uses the pause to take in a breath before bathing those nearest in a deluge of flame. Soldiers who don't collapse where they stand run screaming into their oncoming comrades, spreading fire and chaos within the Arsalian ranks.

The attack broken, Alice and Danahlia shout for Squiggles to give up the fight and take to the air. The dragon clearly wants to continue his battle but with both riders urging him skyward, he grudgingly obeys, leaving his scattered enemies. A few magical bolts continue to follow them up but they're soon out of range.

Safe in the darkening sky, Alice frantically asks, "Danny, are you ok?"

Danahlia shifts, checking herself, "Uh, yup. All bits accounted for. You?"

"Yeah, yeah I'm fine," breathes Alice, then cranes her neck to see the side of Squiggles face, "Squigs, you ok?"

Squiggles grumbles, perhaps upset that he wasn't allowed to finish the battle.

Danahlia grabs Alice around the waist, her chest still heaving, "Well, we ate their commander and set a bunch of 'em on fire. That'll probably hold 'em for a while."

"I hope Lowe wasn't hit by any o' that," says Alice, looking down around Squiggles to the wildly moving fires of burning men and their comrades' torches. She then pans her gaze to the spots of orange torch light coming from the other battalions, still standing firm an oblivious distance away across the foot of the mountains.

Danahlia places her head on Alice's shoulder, "Lookin' forward to that kiss, huh?"

Alice keeps her eyes on the troop formations below, "What?"

"He *is* pretty handsome, especially with those deep, green eyes," Danahlia says dreamily, despite the wind buffeting them.

"His eyes are gray," says Alice, still peering down.

Danahlia grins into Alice's cheek, "So you *do* like 'im."

"What? I didn't... ," Alice says quickly, then amends, "He's a good man. A good sparring partner."

"I bet he is. I bet he-" thunder interrupts whatever Danahlia was about to say. The dragon riders look east to see thick, angry, black clouds in the night sky.

"If it rains, maybe that'll help put out the

fires," says Alice.

"Yeah, then maybe-" another sharper crack resonates from the west, cutting the Liguna off again. They watch, alert for the source of the sound. Part of the nearest mountain shifts. With many more cracks, loud enough to be heard over the swiftly passing air, a single, fairly bare peak begins to break away from the side of the mountain.

It's a slow, ponderous thing that reminds Alice of a particularly old man getting up from a nap. Massive chunks of earth jolt in one spot, causing an avalanche and the shaking of many trees. Then more do the same as if the mountains were sticky and trying to keep hold of their now moving sibling.

"Ticks, she's really doin' it!" Danahlia exclaims, neither having seen Twinkaleni's titan.

Alice watches intently as the mountain begins to split, the side of it pulling away from the rest while beginning to glow the faintest green. She has Squiggles maneuver closer to see the teetering peak has roots. The stubby, reaching appendages form from the crumbling stone around the base of the monolithic earth creature, becoming thicker and longer as they add more stone to themselves. Eventually, they merge into two massive legs held to the earth by enormous jagged feet. Their coming together hoists the majority of the southern face of the mountain up, carrying the behemoth to a stand. The titan scrapes the sky righting itself, a defiant spire of impossible height, it's peak reaching up even past Squiggles' comfortable flight altitude. Once it steadies, it takes a shaky step toward the foot of the mountains.

It's movement causes resounding thuds that echo across the land and through the air. The pair atop their dragon watch in awe at the power of the titan, causing rocks to slide and trees to fall with each thunderous step. Their attention is taken by thin strands of lighting and bright balls of fire flying up to strike it. Bolts and balls hit hard, turning rock to rubble, but they are so minuscule to the overall size of the titan that the damage appears negligible. Alice follows the magical strikes through the smoke back to the Arsalian army's several battalions, mostly appearing as clusters of tiny, orange torch lights in the night. It cheers the dragon riders to see many torches fanning out to the south, a full fifth of the army already fleeing.

The remaining force continues to pelt the titan with azure bolts and fiery balls but the onslaught doesn't even slow it down. The Arsalians don't seem to know where best to strike the living mountain, sending magical shots all over. Once the titan makes it's way to the inferno of the burning forest, orange light mingles and dances with it's green glow, giving it a frightening, otherworldly appearance. This magnifies several times when the flames of the tallest Zalonya trees begin to climb up the titan in thin strands to a spot about midway up, making the earth borne giant appear as if drinking the fire.

After a few of these sips, the titan stops. An orange glow appears were the fire was taken in, looking unsettlingly like the mouth of the gargantuan monster. A few seconds more and something glowing a furious red comes streaking out. It sails toward the nearest of the Arsalian formations but bursts before it can reach them, sending glittering red bits flying into an already burnt section of forest. The titan begins to move again. Thinking this is likely where Twinkaleni and her mages are, Alice has Squiggles race to the ember colored opening.

It turns out to be a cave, it's face pointing

outward to a fairly sheer cliff. Some of the mages are near the edge, guiding the forest's fire into large boulders with waving motions of their arms. The fire is channeled directly into the rocks, somehow being absorbed by them. One they work on begins to glow red, making a high pitched crackling noise. This one is then picked up by the mage's magic and hurled with tremendous force out of the cave mouth and into the general direction of Arsalia's forces. Flying over the cave, Alice watches the boulder burst in mid flight, still unable to make the distance. Sven is peering out and calling directions to the others when a bolt of lightning strikes nearby, forcing the Murin back. More of the Arsalian's start to focus their shots at the mouth, becoming more accurate the closer the titan comes to them.

Alice guides Squiggles down to the cave mouth to peer inside. In the very back is Twinkaleni, still as a statue, her eyes glowing their furious golden glow as she glares out into some middle distance. There are several earth stones piled around her, all alight with grass green auras. She has her hands on the two beside her, green light flowing down into the earth at her feet. The other mages scramble to get more boulders ready for launch from a stock pile of them. They have to use their magic to keep the boulders from rolling around as the titan shifts and trembles with each step. All the mage's eyes glow in various colors with their mana fury.

Alice calls to Sven, "What can we do to help?!"

He looks up at her with his reaching shadowed gaze then back at the others. A fire ball hits the roof of the cave over him and he has to retreat further from the edge. He then shouts up at her, "Guide our shots!" Alice gives him a nod and has Squiggles fly around the titan.

"Ok, how we gonna do that?" wonders Danahlia.

"Um," Alice hesitates, looking around for a solution. The titan is steadily getting further down the mountain and the desperate fire from the Arsalian army is getting more intense, making it difficult to think. Then it hits her. Alice draws Jellybane and spits on the blade. Or tries to. With heavy winds buffeting them from flight and the oncoming storm, her loogie end up U-turning, hitting Danahlia in the face.

"Ugh, UGH! What the tick, Furface?!" the

Liguna exclaims, rubbing it off.

"Sorry," Alice calls back and then licks the flat of her sword.

After a few moments, the blade begins to glow it's pale green. Highly visible in the darkness, Alice brandishes the magical weapon. She has Squiggles fly before the titan's mouth, doing her best to evade shots while pointing her blade at the nearest Arsalian formation. Seeing it, the mages launch another charged boulder in the general direction of the battalion. The fiery missile streaks into the night sky, crackling with the hastily channeled heat energy. It explodes before reaching the Warm Blood force, doing so close enough that it's super heated shards rain down on the left flank. Alice can see some of the soldiers' torches shift about under the attack and more men retreat.

Alice maneuvers Squiggles back into place, giving her sword another lick to direct another shot. This one explodes closer to the Warm Blood formation's center, spreading red hot bits of rock over the clustered men.

Danahlia cheers, "That one got 'em! Whoa!"

Alice has Squiggles bank sharply to avoid a hail of fire balls and lightning bolts the army sends their way. The dragon would likely not be affected much by them but his riders were not nearly so resistant to magic. As they do their best to dodge the magical shots, they can see small fires blossoming among the hit battalion. Dropped torches or charged boulder fragments have likely gotten the tall, dry grasses of the plains to light and soldiers are forced to break formation to avoid the spreading fires.

"If we can get the plains to catch around 'em, the army 'll have to retreat!" Alice calls back to Danahlia.

The Liguna gives her waist a squeeze, "Fight fire with *more* fire. I like it!"

As the titan continues it's lumbering trek, the Arsalian forces move to avoid it while still firing magical bolts in an effort to stop the creature. Alice directs another of the mage's flaming shots, hoping the Warm Blood army will retreat before too much damage is done. Boulder after fiery boulder is launched by the mages, guided by Alice's glowing sword. The oncoming storm's fierce winds aid the catching of the flames and the first struck battalion begins it's retreat in earnest.

Gladdened by the sight of so many tiny torch lights fleeing hungry flames, Alice begins directing shots at the other battalions. It's getting steadily harder to maneuver Squiggles with the winds becoming more powerful. The air is also becoming cool and wet, telling Alice a heavy rain is almost upon them. She knows that if they don't finish this soon, the fires will be doused, saving the mountain forest but taking away any chance of fire breaking the army's resolve.

She needn't worry. After seeing so many of their comrades retreat before the titan, still showing no signs of slowing, a few more shots have the remaining battalions' spirits broken. The magical assault steadily dies off as hundreds of tiny torch lights head back to Arsalia and the safety of its cities. The army had been routed.

Alice and Danahlia cheer, the Liguna even suggesting they have Squiggles burn the plains behind the fleeing Warm Bloods, "Really light a fire under their tails so they don't even think of comin' back!"

Before Alice can consider this, a massive resounding thud takes their attention. They look back to see the titan has dropped to its wide base, embedding itself deep into its mother mountain's side. It's legs lose their shape, piling around it, and a small green light flies out of the titan's mouth over Squiggles. Alice has the dragon turn around to investigate.

Upon reaching the cave they find most of the mages, including Twinkaleni, collapsed on the ground. Sven is one of the few left standing and works to drag the rest to the edge.

Once Squiggles is close enough, the black eyed Murin calls, "We're all but spent. Can you fly us back to the main tunnel?"

"Of course!" Alice calls back, landing Squiggles.

There isn't much room and the dragon half hangs off the cliff, using his powerful claws to dig into the rock and keep steady against the strengthening wind. Alice, Danahlia, Sven, and the mages that can, help get the rest aboard Squiggles. As he's being loaded with passengers, several terrifying crashes of thunder announce the coming storm. Just as they take off, it begins to rain. And hard.

Everyone holds tightly to the net mesh over Squiggles' back, those able needed to help keep the unconscious aboard. Alice holds a limp Twinkaleni in her lap, barely able to see more than a few meters before them in the intense wind and rain. Squiggles grumbles his displeasure at being in this weather as Alice tries to guide him down to the forest canopy. Before they get very far, a massive gust rips Twinkaleni from her arms, sending the small Murin sailing off into the turbulent, night sky. Alice instinctively tries to reach for her only to lose her grip on Squiggles' straps. Before she can react, she's taken by the wind herself and flung over the dragon's side, Danahlia and the mages shouting after them.

Alice flails wildly through the tempestuous air, screaming in horror. As she falls, she catches a glimpse of Twinkaleni's pale, gray fur through the rain and for a mad second tries to reach her, thinking that if Squiggles can dive fast enough he might be able to get to them. But he wouldn't. Danahlia wouldn't let him risk everyone else with such a reckless maneuver. Still, Alice reaches for Twinkaleni's small form, not letting the pointlessness of the act distract her from the effort.

The Murin is just too far. Flashes of lightning show that they're actually falling further away from each other while the many trees of the once great mountain forest, now vengeful charred spikes, are quickly coming to greet them. Alice extends her arms, hooking her fingers with some small hope that she might catch a branch to slow her fall. She looks over one more time before she hits the trees to see Twinkaleni has vanished from sight. Before she can even come up with a thought as to why, a horrible jolt of pain rips through her leg.

She yelps, certain she'd been impaled on a tree, the pain ripping and pulling her leg upward as her body continues to fall. Her leg feels as if it's also being crushed under some tremendous pressure and she looks to see a deeply shadowed winged form over her. Immediately, she thinks it must be Squiggles having grabbed her somehow, but the figure is far too small. Then a flash of lighting reveals her leg to be clutched in the powerful talons of Lolani. The Cloudstalker huntress beats her large, avian wings looking down around Alice, unable to stop her descent but doing what she can to slow it. Breathless from screaming, all Alice can do is look to the ground and brace for the landing.

She's plopped down in the mud, unable to believe she's still alive. Lolani lands nearby and Alice immediately looks around for Twinkaleni, desperately hoping she had somehow been saved as well. She's frantically trying to catch her breath and ask if the Wakuwai woman had seen the Murin when Weiya comes gliding in with the mage in her own talons, having a much easier time with her considerably smaller catch.

The younger huntress excitedly reports, "Saved you again, we did we did we did," then she jeers, "Foolish furries, trying to fly?"

Weiya gets a look from Lolani that silences her and the mature Ornivian leans over Alice to examine the Tokala, "Are you hurt, Drakoda?"

Alice's leg feels like it was pulled from the socket but instead of complaining, she reaches up to hug the hawk woman, tearfully thanking her for saving their lives. After a moment to see Alice's leg isn't quite as bad as it feels, Lolani asks, "Why do the mountains burn?"

Alice crawls over to Twinkaleni and explains what had been happening. The Murin seems fine, still unconscious from commanding the titan but otherwise intact. Squiggles finds them a minute later with Danahlia and the other mages. More Cloudstalkers arrive with them. Weiya says the tribe had just returned from the Azuma Sea, far to the east. They flew above the storm and spotted Twinkaleni's titan, which they thought was one of their mountain gods. They saw Squiggles near it and figured Alice and her friends were likely nearby. Still being heavily rained on, it's decided to head to the mages' last cave in order to discuss what has been happening in Arsalia in greater detail.

The Wakuwai dislike being on the ground and like caves even less, but still prefer them to getting soaked. They stand stoically at the cave mouth, unwilling to go in further, as they are told of the mages' rebellion against the kingdom and the army that had scorched the mountains in an effort to destroy it. The Cloudstalkers seem very skeptical of the still unconscious Twinkaleni's ability to summon forth a living mountain, but their anger with Arsalia for attempting to burn their home is clear. They decide Arsalia has angered the gods with their careless disrespect of the land. The tribe feels this better explains the army's defeat by the earth giant, their gods granting the tiny Murin this power to punish the ground bound Warm Bloods and then wiping away their misdeeds with the storm. No one offers argument.

Lolani, now leader of the Cloudstalkers after Ulima had passed away sometime ago, decides her people will no longer be servants of Arsalia either. Valued as high speed scouts and messengers, generations of her people had been taken to be used in Arsalia as sort of a tribute for allowing the Ornivians to live and hunt on their traditional lands. Too few to fight Arsalia themselves, the proud hunters found themselves unable to refuse. Now, firm in the belief that the Arsalians have angered their gods, Lolani states they will no longer be at the flightless Warm Bloods' beck and call.

Alice, with Danahlia draped around her as the Liguna had been since being recovered, wonders if they'll leave Arsalia like the mages. Lolani assures all that the Cloudstalkers would not be abandoning their ancestral home and if it came to it, they would fight Arsalia to the last warrior. Lolani's people approve of her words, but it worries Alice to hear them. Ulima understood that the Cloudstalkers' survival in the Gadara Mountains relied heavily on the peace between the Wakuwai and the Arsalians. The past elder knew her people had to sacrifice much to maintain their way of life but it was maintained at least. Before the hawk people depart to their winter camp, Alice is sure to tell them that they will be welcome wherever she and the mages settle.

Squiggles again, and more loudly, shares his disinterest in remaining in the rain, being too large to fit in the cave. This prompts the mages to use what little magic they have left to bury the entrance of the last tunnel they know of that leads through the mountains. Their mission complete, the exhausted bunch again board the dragon and once more take to the air. They fly over the Gadara Mountains to meet with their anxiously waiting friends. From there, they begin their journey away from Arsalia's borders, heading north into the unknown Wildlands, and to freedom.

Epilogue

With the threat of elemental attack seemingly over and the Feorians dispersing from its borders, Arsalia is soon gripped by civil war, the powerful and ambitious eager to claim its yet vacant throne. After establishing a base, Alice and her friends are able to make use of the chaos to continue their liberation of the magically gifted still held in the Warm Blood kingdom. They make efforts to locate the freed mages' families, finding many to be eager for the opportunity to reunite with their kin and leave their war torn country behind.

The dark times in Arsalia mean even orphans, despite having no lands or families to fight for, are not free from the call to arms. Those under Kaliska's care are no exception. As warring factions become more desperate, they seek younger and younger boys to fill their depleting ranks. Kaliska's aid is also highly sought, and even demanded. After losing some of her own to the war and enduring various threats, the healer decides the danger has become too great and accepts her friends' invitation to join them in the north. Once there, Kaliska's abilities and teachings make her a very well respected member of the fledgling community.

The moment he is recovered enough from his injuries, Lowe Fenris does find his way back to Alice, determined to win his prize. The Tokala and Lobovan have many duels together and eventually, Lowe manages to earn his sought kiss. Those who saw this last duel still argue if Lowe truly won or Alice threw the battle, but the respect shared between the two is clear. From then on, Alice, Danahlia, and Lowe are often seen in each others company.

Many years of strife pass before word from beyond the border begins to trickle in to war ravaged Arsalia. Unusual stories tell of the rise of a city deep within the vast forests of the Wildlands, farther north than most would ever dare travel. A city most often described as being so abundant with magic that the whole of it glows in the darkest night. A city where stone men are said to walk the streets and build structures higher than even the tallest trees. A city where all races can be seen working together regardless of the blood that flows in their veins. A city said to be under the protection of a great and powerful dragon. A city named Twinkle, after it's founder.

About the Author:

K.J. Bailey (Kenichiro Justin Bailey) has thus far only written the Alice Dippleblack series, but looks forward to creating more fantastical worlds.

www.ingramcontent.com/pod-product-compliance
Lightning Source LLC
Chambersburg PA
CBHW020552180626
46810CB00007B/2476